Welcome to
MY WORLD

Hi! I'm Humphrey. I'm lucky to be
the classroom hamster in Room 26
of Longfellow School. It's a big job
because I have to go home with a
different student each weekend and
try to help my friends. Luckily, my
cage has a lock-that-doesn't-lock,
so I can get out and have
BIG-BIG-BIG adventures!

Have you read all of Humphrey's adventures?

The World According to Humphrey
Friendship According to Humphrey
Trouble According to Humphrey
Adventure According to Humphrey
(special publication for World Book Day 2008)
Surprises According to Humphrey
More Adventures According to Humphrey
Holidays According to Humphrey
School According to Humphrey
Mysteries According to Humphrey
Christmas According to Humphrey
Humphrey's Big-Big-Big Book of Stories
(3 books in 1)
Humphrey's Great-Great-Great Book of Stories
(3 books in 1)
Humphrey's Ho-Ho-Ho Book of Stories
(3 books in 1)

Humphrey's Book of Fun-Fun-Fun
Humphrey's Book of Summer Fun
Humphrey's Book of Christmas Fun

Humphrey's Ha-Ha-Ha Joke Book

Humphrey's World of Pets

Humphrey's Tiny Tales

My Pet Show Panic!
My Treasure Hunt Trouble!
(special publication for World Book Day 2011)
My Summer Fair Surprise!
My Creepy-Crawly Camping Adventure!
My Great Big Birthday Bash!
My Playful Puppy Problem!
My Really Wheely Racing Day!

Bumper Book of Humphrey's Tiny Tales 1

By the same author

The Princess and the Peabodys

Bumper Book of

Humphrey's
Tiny Tales

Book 2

Betty G. Birney

Illustrated by Penny Dann

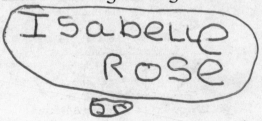

ff

FABER & FABER

First published in this collection in 2014
by Faber and Faber Limited
Bloomsbury House, 74–77
Great Russell Street, London WC1B 3DA

Printed in England by CPI Group (UK) Ltd, Croydon CR0 4YY

A CIP record for this book
is available from the British Library

ISBN 978–0–571–31051–7

FSC
www.fsc.org
MIX
Paper from
responsible sources
FSC® C101712

2 4 6 8 10 9 7 5 3 1

Bumper Book of

Humphrey's
Tiny Tales

Book 2

Betty G. Birney worked at Disneyland and the Disney Studios, has written many children's television shows and is the author of over forty books, including the bestselling *The World According to Humphrey*, which won the Richard and Judy Children's Book Club Award, as well as a further nine books in the *According to Humphrey* series, and eight books in the *Humphrey's Tiny Tales* series. Her work has won many awards, including an Emmy and three Humanitas Prizes. She lives in America with her husband.

Praise for Humphrey:

CONTENTS

My Great Big
BIRTHDAY BASH!

I'd like you to meet some of my friends

Og

a frog, is the other classroom pet in Room 26. He makes a funny sound: BOING!

Mrs Brisbane

is our teacher. She really understands her students – even me!

Lower-Your-Voice-A.J.

has a loud voice and calls me Humphrey Dumpty.

Raise-Your-Hand-Heidi

is always quick with an answer.

Stop-Giggling-Gail

loves to giggle – and so do I!

Repeat-It-Please-Richie

is the caretaker Aldo's nephew and a classmate of mine.

Don't-Complain-Mandy

has a hamster named Winky!

I-Heard-That-Kirk

LOVES-LOVES-LOVES to joke and have fun.

I think you'll like my other friends, too, such as
*Wait-For-The-Bell-Garth, Golden-Miranda,
Sit-Still-Seth* and *Speak-Up-Sayeh.*

CONTENTS

BIRTHDAYS-BIRTHDAYS-BIRTHDAYS

There are lots of exciting things that happen in Room 26 of Longfellow School.

I see them all because I live there. I am the classroom hamster.

But I think the best part of the day is when my friends come bursting through the door in the morning.

'Hi, Humphrey Dumpty!' A.J. always shouts.

A.J. has a LOUD-LOUD-LOUD voice, so I call him Lower-Your-Voice-A.J.

'Hi, A.J.!' I squeak back.

Garth is usually with A.J. because they're best friends.

I call him Wait-For-The-Bell-Garth because he's always out of the door first at the end of the school day.

Then one morning, I-Heard-That-Kirk-Chen came into our classroom and said, 'Happy birthday to me!'

'It's *not* your birthday, Kirk,' Mandy said.

Mandy Payne is a nice girl but she does like to complain.

I call her Don't-Complain-Mandy-Payne.

'It's *almost* my birthday,' Kirk said.
'It will be on Friday.'

Mandy looked up at the row of cupcakes above the chalkboard. She shook her head.

Sometimes when I look at those cupcakes, my tail twitches and my whiskers wiggle.

They look so YUMMY-YUMMY-YUMMY!

The problem is they're not real cupcakes.

They're just pictures of cupcakes with candles on top.

Each one has a name and a date.

The cupcakes help us remember when a classmate has a birthday.

One thing I've learned
from humans – birthdays are
unsqueakably important!

'No, it's not!' I heard Mandy insist
loudly.

Our teacher, Mrs Brisbane, asked,
'What's the problem?'

'Kirk says it's his birthday on
Friday, but it's not.' Mandy pointed
to the cupcakes. 'See? His birthday is
on Saturday.'

Mrs Brisbane nodded. 'Yes. But
since we don't have school on

Saturday, we're celebrating Kirk's birthday on Friday.'

'Fine,' Mandy said. 'But he shouldn't say it's his birthday when it's not.'

'Please Don't-Complain-Mandy-Payne,' Mrs Brisbane said.

'Hey, Mandy, I've got a joke for you,' Kirk said.

He *loves* to tell jokes and I think he wanted to make Mandy smile.

'What do you give a 900-pound gorilla for his birthday?' he asked.

'I don't know,' she answered.

'Anything he wants!' Kirk said, howling with laughter.

Some of my other friends laughed,

too, like Stop-Giggling-Gail, who is always laughing.

'Anything he wants!' Repeat-It-Please-Richie said.

Richie, A.J. and Garth beat their chests and made grunting sounds.

I think they were pretending to be gorillas.

Just then, the bell rang.

School was starting and my friends all sat down.

After Mrs Brisbane took the register, Kirk raised his hand.

'Mrs Brisbane, am I going to be able to take Humphrey home for the weekend like you said?' he asked.

I live in Room 26, but I'm LUCKY-LUCKY-LUCKY that I get to go home with my friends on weekends.

Our teacher nodded. 'Yes, Kirk.'

'Good,' Kirk said. 'He'll be there for my birthday *hsab*. Everyone in class is invited.'

Hsab? What was that strange word?

The way he said it sounded like 'huh–sab'.

Mrs Brisbane looked puzzled.

'I'm glad everyone is invited,' she said. 'But I've never heard of a *hsab* before. What does it mean?'

'I can't tell you!' Kirk grinned broadly. 'H–S–A–B. You have to work it out for yourselves. That's part of the fun.'

Mrs Brisbane wrote the strange word on the board in big letters:

'Maybe if we look at the word, it will help,' she said.

Then she began teaching the class about numbers.

She said something about Jonny having twelve apples and Suzy taking away eight.

I don't know Suzy, but I hope she asked Jonny before she took away his apples!

I tried to pay attention to what Mrs Brisbane was saying, but my mind kept wandering to the word on the board.

Hsab. What on earth could it mean?

Later that night, I asked the other classroom pet, Og the frog, if he'd worked it out.

Og lives in a tank next to my cage on a table by the window.

'BOING-BOING-BOING!' he replied.

He makes a funny sound, but he's really very nice for a frog.

'Me neither,' I said.

I took out the little notebook and

pencil that I keep hidden behind the mirror in my cage.

I wrote down the word so I could take a closer look.

H-S-A-B.

I turned the notebook upside down.

I turned it sideways.

I even turned the notebook backwards.

I couldn't see the word any more.

But I could see the mirror.

In the mirror, everything looks backwards, including words.

This word looked STRANGE-STRANGE-STRANGE.

I saw a backwards B, an A, a backwards S and an H.

If the backwards letters were

forwards, the word would be
B-A-S-H!

A bash! A bash is like a great, big
wonderful party.

So Kirk was having a birthday
bash!

But why did he write the word
backwards?

Humans are nice, but sometimes they do very strange things.

I wasn't the only one in Room 26 who had worked out that *hsab* was bash spelled backwards.

'It's a birthday bash,' A.J. shouted as he came into class the next morning. 'I got the invitation and my mum held it up to the mirror. Some of the letters were backwards, but she worked it out.'

A.J.'s mum must be SMART-SMART-SMART (like me).

Mrs Brisbane asked Kirk to explain why he had written the word backwards.

'It's a backwards party,'
he said. 'Everything will be
backwards. Hands up if you're
coming.'

Every hand in the room shot
up.

My paw went up, too.

'It sounds like a very interesting party,' Mrs Brisbane said.

'Mrs Brisbane?' Mandy said. 'I've been looking at the birthday cupcakes and some names are missing.'

Our teacher looked up at the row of cupcakes.

'Yours isn't up there,' Mandy continued. 'Or Humphrey's.'

I scrambled up to the tippy-top of my cage to see if she was right.

Sure enough, Mrs Brisbane's name wasn't there and neither was mine.

Another name was also missing.

'What about Og?' I squeaked at the top of my tiny lungs.

'Ooh, Og's missing, too,' Raise-Your-Hand-Heidi said.

As usual, she forgot to raise her hand.

When I squeak, humans can't understand me, so I was glad that Heidi had also noticed that Og's name was missing.

'I don't need everyone to remember my birthday,' Mrs Brisbane said. 'Every day I'm here in Room 26 is a special day for me.'

My friends still wanted to know about Og and me.

'The problem is, I don't know when they were born,' Mrs Brisbane said.

I suddenly felt
SAD–SAD–SAD.

If no one knew
when I was born, I
could never have a
birthday!

Heidi said, 'Frogs aren't born.
They're hatched!'

'That's right,' Mrs Brisbane said.
'Frogs start out as eggs.'

Og splashed around a little in his
tank.

I felt SAD–SAD–SAD for him, too.

He could never have a birthday.

And though he could have a
hatch-day, nobody knew when it
was.

A SILLY-SILLY-SILLY Party

On Friday, we celebrated Kirk's birthday in class.

First, he got to wear the paper birthday crown all day.

Next, he got to pick a gift from Mrs Brisbane's birthday grab bag.

She asked him to close his eyes and reach inside.

The birthday surprise he pulled out was a big sheet of silly stickers.

I was glad it was something funny, since Kirk likes to joke around.

Then we all sang him a birthday song.

I happily squeaked along and I even heard a few BOING-BOINGS coming from Og.

At the end of the day, Kirk's mum came to pick us up.

'Bye, Og,' I squeaked. 'I'll tell you all about the bash on Monday.'

Og doesn't leave Room 26 at the weekends, because he can go a few days without being fed.

I didn't like leaving him behind.

He didn't have his own hatch-day *and* he wasn't going to Kirk's birthday bash.

I guess it's not easy being a frog.

The next day, when it was time for the party, Kirk set me on a big table near the front door so I could see everything.

'Just watch, Humphrey,' he said. 'The fun is about to begin.'

And something funny had already begun because Kirk had his shirt on back to front so the buttons went down his back!

Most of his clothes were on back to front, except his shoes.

I think it would be hard for a human to walk in back-to-front shoes.

The doorbell rang and Kirk ran to open it.

'Goodbye,' he said as Richie entered.

Kirk turned Richie around and said, 'Not like that! You have to come in backwards.'

So Richie came through the door again, walking backwards.

He wasn't just walking backwards.

He was also wearing his clothes inside out!

Because it was a backwards party, all my friends from Room 26 arrived wearing their clothes back to front or inside out.

Everyone loved the birthday balloons, which were attached to the floor instead of the ceiling.

And they laughed at the music, which sounded STRANGE-STRANGE-STRANGE because it was playing backwards.

Then my friends had a relay race in the garden.

It was unsqueakably funny to see them running backwards.

My friends laughed, too.

One nice thing about humans is that they can laugh at themselves.

At last, it was time to eat.

Kirk moved my cage to a little table near the big table where all my friends were gathered.

Kirk's mum brought in the birthday cake.

On top, were bright red icing letters: KRIK, YADHTRIB YPPAH.

I had a pretty good idea that those letters spelled out: HAPPY BIRTHDAY, KIRK – only backwards!

Singing the birthday song backwards wasn't easy but Kirk's

dad had printed out the words so everyone could take part.

Then, instead of blowing out his birthday candles, Kirk helped his mum light them.

'Make a wish,' Kirk's mum said.

Kirk closed his eyes and opened them again.

Then he blew out the candles.

But the funny thing was, they lit right up again!

Kirk tried to blow them out again and again, but they kept relighting because they were trick candles.

'Backwards candles,' Kirk said. 'Funny!'

Finally, Kirk's dad put them out.

Then, Kirk's mum served ice cream.

'Hey, what did the ice cream say to the cake?' Kirk asked.

No one answered, so Kirk said, 'What's eating you?'

I laughed and laughed – it was such a funny joke!

Kirk's friends gave him presents wrapped in inside-out paper with bows tied on the bottom instead of the top.

He got a toy helicopter, some rocks for his rock collection, a board game and a joke book.

I think the joke book was his favourite present because he started reading it right away.

'Hey, what does a cat eat for his birthday?' he asked. '*Mice* cream and cake!'

Everybody laughed except me.

After all, mice and hamsters are a lot alike.

I was SO-SO-SO embarrassed that I didn't have a present for Kirk.

But then I had an idea.

I may not have had a present, but at least I could add something to the party.

I decided to put on a show.

First, I started spinning on my wheel.

The sound got Richie's attention.

'Hey, look at Humphrey go!' he said.

Soon, all my friends were gathered around my cage, watching.

I hopped off my wheel and climbed up the big tree branch in my cage, all the way to the top.

'Oooh,' my friends said.

Then I grabbed on to
the top bars and hung
on tightly.

Slowly and
carefully, I made
my way across the
top of the cage.

'Ahhh!' my
friends said.

To finish off the
act, I made a daring
jump straight down
and landed in my
bedding.

I hadn't planned
to do a double-flip,
but when I did, my

friends all clapped.

When it was time for the guests to leave, everyone said 'Hello,' which made me giggle.

'Hello!' I squeaked loudly.

After everyone had gone home, Kirk said, 'Thank you, Humphrey, for helping make my party turn out so well!'

'Thanks for inviting me,' I squeaked back.

I don't think I'd ever had so much fun in my life.

I only wished Og could have been there, too.

When I got back to Room 26 on Monday morning, I was about to tell my froggy friend about the backwards bash when I heard Garth say, 'Listen up, everybody.'

He looked over at my cage.

Then he glanced at the door, where Mrs Brisbane was talking to the teacher across the hall.

'I have a great idea. Want to hear

it?' Garth asked in a loud whisper.

'Yes!' the other students yelled.

'YES-YES-YES!' I squeaked.

'Sssh,' he said. 'It's a secret. Listen up.'

Garth turned to Richie and whispered something in his ear.

All I could hear were the words *'surprise'* and *'Thursday'*.

I like surprises and wanted to hear more.

'Could you squeak up just a little?' I asked.

Richie turned to Miranda and whispered in her ear.

I perked up my tiny pink ears but all I could hear was the word '*present*'.

Miranda smiled. 'Oooh, I have an idea!'

'Sssh,' the other children told her.

'Sorry,' Miranda said.

Then Miranda turned to Gail and whispered in her ear.

Gail giggled, then whispered in
A.J.'s ear.

This time, I heard the word 'birthday'.
Next, A.J. whispered in Kirk's ear.

A.J.'s voice is so loud, even when he
whispers, A.J. is loud.

I couldn't hear everything he said
but I did hear him say 'Mrs Brisbane'.

So that was the secret!

They were having a surprise
birthday party for Mrs Brisbane on
Thursday!

My whiskers wiggled at the exciting news.

But I wished my friends had whispered in my ear, too, so I'd know more about the plans.

Mrs Brisbane came over to the group.

'Why are you all whispering?' she asked.

'It's a secret,' A.J. said.

Mrs Brisbane smiled. 'As long as it's a good secret, I guess that's okay.'

She glanced over at my cage and said, 'Isn't that right, Humphrey?'

I wasn't sure if secrets were ever okay.

Before I could answer, the bell rang and Mrs Brisbane started class.

I always try to listen to every word she says.

But it wasn't easy to listen when my mind was racing with thoughts about Mrs Brisbane's surprise birthday party.

Would it be backwards or forwards?

Would there be games?

And most importantly, would there be cake?

Cake is *unsqueakably* important at a birthday party.

A GREAT-GREAT-GREAT
Escape

The next few days I was pawsitively
happy all the time.

I'd watch Mrs Brisbane teaching
and think about how happy she'd be
on Thursday when the whole class
shouted, 'Surprise!'

I'd hear my friends whispering
about 'presents' and I'd think about

how she'd smile when she opened her gifts.

I even practised the birthday song in my mirror.

This time, I squeaked it forwards, not backwards.

I *was* puzzled by a few things that happened during the week.

On Tuesday, Sayeh and Seth suddenly started measuring my cage with a ruler.

They also measured Og's tank.

'It's for a maths problem,' Sayeh said.

Sometimes, Mrs Brisbane has students measure things for maths, so that made sense.

On Wednesday, when my friends
worked on an art project, Mandy
raised her hand and asked how to
spell my name.

Mrs Brisbane wrote, 'Humphrey'
on the board.

She also let the students work a lot
longer than usual on their art.

Even though hamsters like me are often awake at night, on Wednesday night, I thought I should get some sleep.

After all, I wanted to be wide awake for Mrs Brisbane's surprise birthday party the next day.

I dozed for a while and I had a very strange dream.

First I dreamed about YUMMY-YUMMY-YUMMY dancing cupcakes.

Then I dreamed about the look
on Mrs Brisbane's face when she
saw her gifts and cake and we all
squeaked 'Happy Birthday' to her.

Suddenly I woke
up with a terrible
thought.

'Og!' I squeaked.
'We forgot
something.'

Og splashed around in his tank.

I jiggled the lock on my cage door.

It seemed tightly locked, but I have
a secret way to open it.

That's why I call it the lock-that-
doesn't-lock.

I jiggled the lock some more.

When it opened, I was free!

I hurried across the table to Og's tank.

'Og, we forgot to get a present for Mrs Brisbane!' I told him. 'Just like I forgot to get one for Kirk!'

'BOING-BOING-BOING!' he answered excitedly.

'We have to give her something so she'll know we're glad she's our teacher,' I explained. 'But what?'

Og stared at me from his tank, but he didn't answer.

I guessed it was up to me to think of an idea.

We couldn't go to the shops to buy something, so we'd have to make her a gift.

I looked up at the chalkboard, with the row of cupcakes around it.

'I know,' I said. 'Let's make her a cake. After all, you can't have too much cake at a birthday party!'

'BOING-BOING-BOING!' Og hopped up and down.

'Of course, we can't *bake* a cake,'
I said. 'But we can make her a
hamster-and-frog kind of cake.'

'BOING!' Og agreed.

I went back into my cage and was
delighted to see that my food dish
was full of crunchy Nutri-Nibbles.

It's one of my favourite treats.

One by one, I put a few Nutri-
Nibbles in my cheek pouch, carried
them out of the cage, and set them
down in front of Og's tank.

After a while I had a nice stack of
them.

Nutri-Nibbles are
a little too crunchy
to make a cake.

'I need your help, Og,' I said.

'BOING-BOING!' he answered.

'Splash a lot of water so it goes on the Nutri-Nibbles,' I said.

Then I scampered out of the way, because water isn't good for hamsters.

Og splashed . . . and splashed some more.

His tank has a top, but if he splashes hard enough, some of the water spills out of the crack at the top.

Soon, the pile of Nutri-Nibbles was nice and wet.

'Thanks, Og,' I said.

Then I went straight to work, using my paws to pat and smooth the Nutri-Nibbles batter into a circle.

'It *looks* like a cake,' I said. 'But it's awfully plain.'

'BOING-BOING,' Og agreed.

So I went back into the cage and dug around in my bedding, where

sometimes I store food.

I found two strawberries and three raisins and pressed them into the side of the cake.

Next, I scurried to the back of the table where Mrs Brisbane keeps food and supplies for Og and me.

There were big bags of Mighty Mealworms, Healthy Dots, Nutri-Nibbles, Hamster Chew-Chews and nice soft hay. Yum!

There was also a box of Og's Froggy Fish Sticks and a can of crickets!

Yep, that's what frogs eat. Eww!

I chewed a small hole in the bag of hay and made several trips back and forth to the cake.

Soon it had a nice frosting of soft hay on top.

Then I added a Chew-Chew, which almost looked like a candle.

'BOING-BOING-BOING!' Og said. 'BOING-BOING-BOING-*BOING!*'

I thought the cake looked great, but Og seemed a little *too* excited about it.

'Just one more thing,' I told him. 'I think a few Healthy Dots would look nice.'

Healthy Dots are good for hamsters, but they also come in lots of colours and look like sweets.

Og splashed crazily in his tank, but I scurried to the back of the table once again.

I was trying to work out how to open the box when I heard people talking.

'BOING-BOING-*BOING*!' Og twanged.

I couldn't see anything, but when I heard A.J.'s loud voice, I knew my friends had come into the classroom.

I looked up at the window.

It was already light outside!

I heard Mrs Brisbane saying, 'Good morning.'

I heard the bell ring, too.

The school day was starting!

It was the first time I wasn't in my cage when my friends were in the room.

I was STUCK-STUCK-STUCK.

A BIG - BIG - BIG Surprise

Mrs Brisbane took the register.

Then I heard Heidi say, 'Can we do it now?'

Heidi sounded unsqueakably excited.

'I think we should wait until just before break,' Mrs Brisbane said.

I could hear more talking, but I

couldn't understand it all.

I can hear fine in my cage, but from my hiding place behind Healthy Dots, the sounds were muffled.

If only I could see what was going on!

I thought I heard Garth ask, 'Where's Humphrey? I don't see him.'

Then Mrs Brisbane said something about me making a map.

Or maybe she said I was taking a nap.

I would have been so happy to be taking a nap instead of being stuck outside my cage.

I wasn't exactly sure what would happen next.

Maybe my friends would discover I was missing and find out about the lock-that-doesn't-lock.

If they fixed it, I'd be trapped in my cage for ever!

Or, maybe no one would notice I

wasn't in my cage and I'd miss out
on Mrs Brisbane's birthday party!

I didn't like either of those ideas
one bit.

Og splashed nervously in his tank.

I crossed my toes and hoped that
everyone would leave the classroom
so I could return to my cage.

Or at least that my friends would

get so busy they wouldn't notice me sneaking back.

Then I heard Mrs Brisbane say, 'It's time.'

Which was odd, because the birthday party was supposed to be a surprise for her.

Next, I heard lots of whispering and rustling.

I heard footsteps moving closer and closer.

I heard Gail giggle and someone said, 'Sssh!'

Then Mrs Brisbane whispered, 'Ready?'

Suddenly, all of my classmates screamed, 'SURPRISE!'

'Come on out, Humphrey Dumpty,' A.J. shouted. 'It's time for your birthday party!'

Sayeh's softer voice said, 'And Og's hatch-day party.'

'BOING!' Og said.

My birthday party? Og's hatch-day party?

I was amazed.

The surprise party wasn't for Mrs Brisbane.

The surprise party was for Og and me.

But the biggest surprise was the fact that I was missing my own celebration!

'Where is he?' Richie asked.

Og splashed wildly.

I think he was as confused as I was.

'Come on out, Humphrey. We want to wish you Happy Birthday,' Mrs Brisbane said.

I didn't know what to do, so I sat and waited.

Then Mrs Brisbane told someone to open the cage and a few seconds later, I heard Garth say, 'He's not here!'

Of course, everyone thought that was impossible.

There were more rustling noises.

'You're right,' Mrs Brisbane said. 'I don't think Humphrey's in his cage. I wonder if someone left the door unlocked. Or maybe it's broken.'

I heard the cage door open and shut a few times.

'No, Mrs Brisbane,' Art said. 'It works just fine.'

'We must all look for him,' Mrs Brisbane said. 'But we'll have to be very careful not to step on him.'

'Eeek!' I squeaked.

I didn't mean to say it, but just thinking of someone stepping on me, it came out.

'I can hear him!' Miranda said.

Oops!

There was no hiding now, so I decided it was time to show myself.

'Surprise!' I squeaked as I scurried across the table.

'There's Humphrey Dumpty!' A.J. shouted.

Mrs Brisbane scooped me up and put me back in my cage.

'Humphrey, when your friends told me they wanted to give you a surprise party, I never dreamed you wouldn't show up for it,' she said.

So, Mrs Brisbane was in on it all along!

'I don't know how you got out, but please don't do it again,' she said to me.

I didn't squeak back to her, but I was pretty sure I *would* get out of my cage again.

Only next time, I wouldn't get caught!

After that, I had an unsqueakably wonderful time!

Sayeh put a paper birthday crown on top of my cage.

Richie put a paper birthday crown on top of Og's tank.

Then they put a big banner across
my cage, which said, 'HAPPY
BIRTHDAY HUMPHREY!'

So *that's* why they measured my
cage.

Another banner went across Og's
tank.

It said, 'HAPPY HATCH-DAY OG!'

That was their art project.

And they gave us presents.

Og got a special rock that he could climb over or hide under.

And I got something amazing – a tiny bell that makes an unsqueakably nice tinkling sound when I touch it.

It was the BEST-BEST-BEST
present I could imagine!

But my ears
perked up when
I heard A.J.'s loud
voice say, 'Cake
time!'

'It looks as
if Humphrey
already has one,' Mrs Brisbane said,
leaning down to look at the tiny cake
I had made.

'Who made this cute little cake?'
she asked.

No one answered, so I decided to
squeak up.

'I did,' I said. 'I made it for you.'

Mrs Brisbane laughed.

'I guess it's a secret,' she said. 'But Humphrey seems to know who it was.'

I DID-DID-DID!

Then I was presented with the most beautiful cake I've ever seen.

It was made of nuts and seeds and raisins – all my favourite foods!

The whole class sang the Happy
Birthday song to me.

Then they gave Og a cake made
of things he likes and sang a Happy

Hatch-day song to him.

He splashed around happily when
they put it in his tank.

★

At the end of the day, when all my friends had left, Mrs Brisbane came over to our table.

'I hope you liked your party,' she said.

'It was unsqueakably wonderful,' I answered. 'But it was supposed to be for *you*!'

I know that all she heard was SQUEAK-SQUEAK-SQUEAK.

But Mrs Brisbane laughed and said, 'Happy Birthday, Humphrey and Og.'

I said, 'Happy Birthday, Mrs Brisbane.'

Og said, 'BOING-BOING-BOING!'

We both agreed it really was the best birthday bash ever.

I was surprised that the party was for us and not Mrs Brisbane.

And my *friends* were surprised that I wasn't around for my own party.

'I hope we have another birthday and hatch-day party next year,' I told Og when we were alone for the night.

'And I still hope we have a surprise birthday party for Mrs Brisbane,' I added.

'BOING-BOING!' he said.

And then I rang my bell a few more times, just for fun.

My Treasure Hunt
TROUBLE!

I'd like you to meet some of my friends

Og

a frog, is the other classroom pet in Room 26. He makes a funny sound: BOING!

Lower-Your-Voice-A.J.

has a loud voice and calls me Humphrey Dumpty.

Wait-For-The-Bell Garth

is A.J.'s best friend – and a great friend of mine, too!

Andy

Garth's little brother. He calls me 'ham'.

Golden-Miranda

has golden hair, like I do. She also has a dog named Clem. Eeek!

Speak-Up-Sayeh

is unsqueakably smart, but she's shy and doesn't like to speak in class.

Stop-Giggling-Gail

loves to giggle – and so do I!

Sit-Still-Seth

is always on the move.

I think you'll like my other friends, too, such as *Repeat-It-Please-Richie, Pay-Attention-Art, Raise-Your-Hand-Heidi* and *Don't-Complain-Mandy*.

CONTENTS

Secret Treasure

'Can you keep a secret, Humphrey?'
Garth whispered.

'Of course,' I whispered back.

But since I'm a hamster and
Garth is a human, all he heard was
'Squeak!'

'How about you, Og?' Garth asked
my friend.

Og answered 'BOING!' because he

is a frog who makes a VERY-VERY-VERY strange sound.

'There's going to be a treasure hunt in my garden tomorrow,' Garth said. 'But it's a secret. Don't tell anybody, okay?'

'Eeek!' I squeaked. I wasn't sure what a treasure hunt was, but it sounded exciting.

'BOING-BOING!' Og splashed around in his tank.

'I've worked out some of the clues already,' Garth said. 'And I haven't even told A.J.'

A.J. was Garth's best friend. They were both in my class at Longfellow School.

I'm the classroom hamster in
Room 26. Og is the classroom frog.

It's part of my job to go home with
a different student each weekend.

Frogs can go for several days
without food, so Og usually stays
back in Room 26. But this weekend
Garth invited everyone in our class
to a party, including Og and me.
Our teacher, Mrs Brisbane, said
we could both go, which made me
unsqueakably happy.

My cage and Og's tank sat on the
desk in Garth's room. We watched as
he cut paper into squares.

'The clues should be hard,' he
said. 'But not too hard. After all,

somebody has to find the treasure.'

'What's the treasure?' I asked,
wishing Garth could understand me.

Garth stopped cutting paper and
looked at me.

'Thanks, Humphrey,' he said. 'You gave me an idea for a great place to hide it!'

'You're welcome,' I squeaked. 'But what *is* the treasure?'

'BOING!' Og said.

As Garth began writing on the squares of paper, I thought about TREASURE-TREASURE-TREASURE! I knew that treasure was something special, like gold and silver coins. Or sparkly jewels.

In the books Mrs Brisbane read to us in class, people were always looking for treasure. Sometimes treasure was buried in the ground. Sometimes it was at the bottom of the sea.

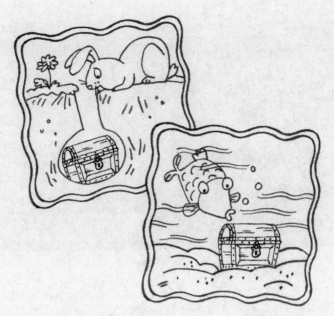

I scurried to the side of my cage near Og's tank.

'What kind of treasure would you like?' I asked him.

Og just stared at me with his goofy eyes. I didn't think coins or jewels would be of much use to a frog. He'd probably rather have crickets or flies. *Ewww!*

Coins or jewels wouldn't be of use to
a hamster, either, but I still wanted to
go on the treasure hunt.

Suddenly, a small voice called out,
'Ham!'

Garth's little brother, Andy, raced
into the room and headed for my cage.

'He's a hamster, not a ham,' Garth
said.

'Ham!' Andy shouted.

I don't like being called a 'ham', but,
to be fair, Andy is quite small.

Andy pointed at the squares of
paper. 'What's that?'

'That's where I'm writing down
clues for the treasure hunt,' Garth
explained.

'What's that?' Andy asked.

'It's a game where my friends have
to follow clues and see who can find

the treasure first,' Garth said.

'What's that?' Andy asked, pointing at Og.

'That's Og the frog,' Garth said. 'Now be quiet so I can write out the clues.'

'What's—' said Andy.

Garth put his finger to his lips and said, 'Sssh!'

Andy put his finger to his lips and said, 'Sssh!' too.

Garth wrote something on one of the squares.

'Frog,' Andy said.

He stared hard at Og. Og stared right back.

'BOING!' Og said in his funny voice.

'Sssh!' Andy said.

Og leaped into the water with a huge splash.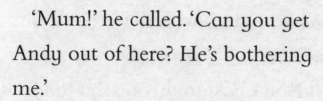

Garth sighed.

'Mum!' he called. 'Can you get Andy out of here? He's bothering me.'

Garth's mum appeared at the door. 'Let Andy help. He wants to be included in the party.'

'I can't write out the clues with him here,' Garth complained.

'You can only stay if you watch quietly,' Garth's mum told Andy.

She put her finger to her lips and said, 'Sssh!'

'Okay,' the little boy answered. 'Sssh!'

At first, Andy watched quietly as Garth began writing on the slips of paper.

'What rhymes with flower?' Garth asked.

'BOING!' Og said.

Poor Og. Doesn't he know that BOING doesn't rhyme with flower at all?

'Shower! That works,' Garth said.

I was trying to think of a flower that showered when Andy asked, 'What's that?'

'A clue,' Garth told him. 'Like a riddle.'

'Widdle,' Andy said.

Aha! A clue is like a riddle! I like riddles. I was unsqueakably curious about these clues.

Garth wrote some more and then asked me, 'What do you think of this clue?' and he read it out loud:

'Everyone knows you must water a flower. Tip me over, I'll give it a shower.'

'GREAT-GREAT-GREAT!' I squeaked. I had no idea what the answer to the riddle was.

As Garth wrote, he muttered other strange words, like 'frown' and 'goal' and 'basket'.

Then he opened a desk drawer and pulled out a treasure chest so small that he could hold it in the palm of his hand. Still, it looked like a real treasure chest and it even had a tiny lock on it.

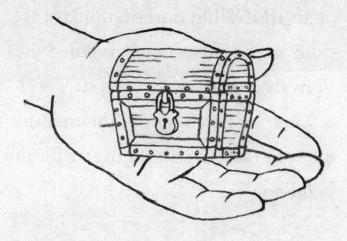

'What's that?' Andy said.

'It's the treasure for the treasure hunt. It's something anyone in Room 26 would love to have,' Garth said.

Anyone? Even a hamster?

'Remember, this is a secret,' he

added. 'Do you promise not to tell anyone?'

'Promise,' Andy said.

'Promise,' I squeaked.

'BOING!' Og agreed.

To my surprise, Garth opened the door to my cage!

Then he carefully put the treasure chest inside, covering it over with my bedding.

'You leave it right there, Humphrey,' he said. 'And don't peek.'

'Okay,' I promised.

But even as I said it, I knew it would be a hard promise to keep.

The Trouble Begins

'A.J.'s here,' Garth's dad called from the hallway.

Garth quickly hid all of the pieces of paper in his desk drawer.

'He's spending the night,' he explained. 'But don't tell him about the treasure hunt.'

'Okay,' Andy said. 'Sssh!'

A.J. raced into the room. 'Hi,

Humphrey Dumpty,' he said.

He calls me Humphrey Dumpty
for fun.

I call him Lower-Your-Voice-A.J.
because of his loud voice.

'Hi, Og,' A.J. said.

Og answered with a friendly,
'BOING!'

'BOING-BOING!'
Andy said.
Then he hopped
across the room,
shouting, 'BOING-
BOING! I'M A FROG!'

'Quiet, Andy,' Garth told him.

A.J. leaned down close to Andy and said, 'Sssh!'

Andy said, 'Sssh!'

'Bedtime, Andy,' Garth's dad called from the hallway.

Andy said, 'Night-night, ham and frog.'

The boys played a game until Garth's dad called from the hallway again.

'Time to get washed and ready for bed, guys,' he said. 'You've got a big day tomorrow.'

Once Garth and A.J. had left, I told Og, 'We've got a big day tomorrow, too.'

This time, Og was silent.

Maybe he wished the treasure was in his tank instead of my cage.

I wanted to uncover the treasure to see what was inside, but I'd promised Garth I wouldn't peek.

It's always a good idea to keep a promise. I hopped on my wheel so I wouldn't think about the treasure.

I was spinning FAST-
FAST-FAST when I saw
the door to my cage open.

I wanted to see who was
opening it, but my wheel was
going so fast, I had to wait
until it slowed down. While
I waited, I saw the shadowy
shape of a hand reach in and
poke around the cage.

I had to see whose hand it
was, so I hopped off the wheel
and flipped head-over-paws
across my bedding.

I must have been dizzy
because everything was still
spinning.

The hand picked up the small treasure chest. I tried to see whose hand it was, but now the chest blocked my view.

'Stop!' I squeaked as loudly as a small hamster can squeak. 'Stop right now!'

'Sssh!' was the only answer.

'Stop, thief!' I squeaked as my heart went THUMP-THUMP-THUMP.

No one answered. But I did smell something. Was it . . . chocolate?

'BOING-BOING!' Og called out as he splashed wildly in his tank.

Before I knew it, the hand had taken the treasure chest out of my cage and closed the door. I dashed forward to see who it was but it was too late. Garth's room was empty.

'Og, did you see the thief?' I asked.

Og didn't answer this time. I don't think he'd seen who it was. Neither had I.

I was unsqueakably upset.

The treasure chest was GONE-GONE-GONE!

★

'A thief was here!' I told Garth when he and A.J. came back, ready for bed. 'We have to find the thief!'

'Calm down, Humphrey Dumpty,' A.J. said. 'Sssh!'

'Goodnight, Humphrey,' Garth said.

He took off his glasses and got into his bed. A.J. got into the other bed in Garth's room.

'BOING–BOING!' Og said.

'Goodnight, Og,' Garth said.

I love humans but sometimes I wish they'd pay a little more attention.

The boys talked in the dark for a while. And soon I could tell by their breathing that they were asleep. But *I* didn't sleep the whole night.

Like most hamsters, I am usually wide awake at night. But I'm not usually so WORRIED-WORRIED-WORRIED.

It had been nice to have the treasure chest in my cage. But it was *not nice at all* to have it missing.

I imagined what would happen the next day. Everyone would try to find out where the treasure was by reading Garth's clues. One of my friends would be the first to get to my cage. But when that friend got there, the treasure would be missing.

I thought about how the winner would be disappointed.

I thought about how Garth would be disappointed.

Garth's parents would be disappointed, too.

But nobody would be more disappointed than me.

Early the next morning, Garth woke up A.J.

'Come on,' he said. 'We've got to get ready for the party. I've got a big surprise planned.'

'What is it?' A.J. asked.

'Wait and see,' Garth said.

Later, while A.J. was out of the room, I tried to tell Garth again that the treasure was missing.

'You sound excited, Humphrey,' he said. 'So am I! After all, you're the most important guest because you have the treasure!'

Except, of course, I hadn't.

The boys went downstairs to get ready for the party. 'I've got to do something, don't you think?' I asked Og.

'BOING-BOING-BOING!' he agreed.

Since the family was at home, I didn't dare go far from my cage. I decided to search for *new* treasure so the party wouldn't be ruined.

It's a secret, but I have a lock-that-doesn't-lock on my cage door. I can get in and out without any humans knowing it.

I jiggled the lock and the door opened. I was free!

It's a LONG-LONG-LONG way down to the floor for a small hamster and I didn't have much time. So I decided to stay close to my cage and explore the top of Garth's desk first.

There was a *lot* to see

on the top of Garth's desk.

The first thing I saw was a cup full of pencils. But these weren't plain pencils. They had amazing things on top, like an orange pumpkin head, a smiling monkey, a shiny star. One pencil looked like a rocket ship!

Next to the pencil cup was a huge yellow smiling face. When I saw it, I smiled back.

'Hello,' I said, trying to be friendly.

Then I saw that the smiling face was really a clock.

'Never mind!' I said.

Behind the clock was a frame made of twigs with a picture of Garth and A.J. in it.

I wandered past a deck of cards and ran right into a tiny pink pig. The pig fell over and let out an 'Oink!'

'Sorry,' I said, and quickly moved on.

There were pads of paper, a large

blue feather and a pencil box with
the planets on it. I know about
planets from our lessons in Room 26.

I kept on walking and found
myself face to face with a row
of big dinosaurs with very large
teeth. They weren't real dinosaurs,
thank goodness. But they still were
unsqueakably scary to a small
hamster like me.

I scurried past a row of toy cars in bright colours. One was painted a shiny red and had no roof. It was just my size and I stopped to look at it.

I just touched the shiny red car with my paw when, suddenly, it lurched forward.

'VROOOM!' the car roared.

'Eeek!' I squeaked.

The car zipped across the desk, making wild turns. I ran for my life, zig-zagging ahead of it until I saw I was running straight towards the end of the desk! And it was a LONG-

LONG-LONG way
down to the floor.

To my left, was a
pencil case that was
taller than I am.

To my right, was the
front edge of the desk.
Eeek!

At the last second, I leaped up onto the pencil case. The car zoomed past me and flew off the end of the desk. It sailed through the air and then landed on Garth's soft bed.

'BOING-BOING!' Og said as I caught my breath.

My heart was pounding, but I told him, 'Don't worry. I'm fine and so is the car!'

'BOING-BOING-BOING!' Og warned me.

He was right. I didn't have much time.

'I'll hurry,' I told him.

Then something caught my eye. Something shiny and gold, like treasure. It was a coin!

I hopped off the pencil case and scampered towards it. When I sniffed it, I realised that it wasn't a real coin, but a chocolate wrapped in gold paper.

Still, it was shiny and gold and my friends all like chocolate.

I held it in my mouth, careful not
to bite down and make teeth marks,
and hurried back to my cage.

Og splashed loudly and called out,
'BOING-BOING!'

'I'll tell you all about it,' I said. But
I didn't have time because I heard
footsteps.

I dashed inside my cage and pulled
the door closed behind me.

I slipped the chocolate coin under

my bedding just as Garth came in.

'Time to go downstairs,' Garth said. 'The party's about to start.'

The Hunt Is On

Garth and his dad carried my cage
and Og's tank outside to a table
under a large umbrella.

'A.J., could you come and help me
ice the cake?' Garth's mum asked.
'You can lick the spoon.'

'Yes, ma'am!' A.J. followed her in to
the house.

Once he was gone, Garth said,

'We have to hide the clues before he comes back.'

Og and I watched as Garth and his dad put the little squares of paper all round the garden.

They put them in odd places, like a watering can and a little red wagon.

'Hurry, Dad,' Garth said.

Suddenly, I heard happy voices. My friends from Room 26 had arrived!

'Oh, Humphrey, I'm so glad you're here!' That was the voice of Miranda Golden. I thought of her as Golden–Miranda because her hair was as golden as my fur.

'Hi, Humphrey! Hi, Og!' a giggly voice said. That had to be Stop-Giggling-Gail. It was hard for her to stop giggling once she got started.

'HI-HI-HI!' I answered.

Once the guests had arrived, Garth's mum called them into the garden for a funny race. First, each of my friends stood in a sack. Then they had to hold on to the sack while they hopped to the finish line.

I wish Og could have been in that race. He's GREAT-GREAT-GREAT at hopping.

But Gail and her friend Heidi
Hopper were good at hopping, too.
They won the race.

Next, my friends split up into pairs
and Garth's parents tied one kid's
right leg to the other kid's left leg.
Then they had to work together
to run to the finish line. It was

unsqueakably funny to see them try to run like that!

Seth and Tabitha won. They are good friends who are both good at sport.

There were other games, too, but it was hard for me to enjoy them. All I could think about was the treasure hunt.

Finally, Garth announced that the hunt would begin. 'There's *real treasure* for the first person who finds it,' he explained.

That was true. It just wasn't the treasure Garth had planned on.

Garth read out the first clue. 'Everyone knows you must water a flower. Tip me over, I'll give it a shower.'

My friends raced off in different directions.

'Og, I saw him put a clue in the watering can,' I squeaked. 'That must be it.'

I was right. Mandy, Richie and Seth all ran to the watering can at the same time.

Mandy reached in and pulled out the next clue.

'The sun is hot, as you will see. You'll be cooler under me.'

There were squeals of excitement as everyone raced to the umbrella over the table I was on.

A.J. had to stand on a chair to reach the next clue and read it.

'You'll find that you will never frown. If you let me go up and down.'

It took a little longer this time for my friends to solve that riddle, but I quickly got it.

'The swing!' I squeaked.

I don't think they understood me, but they all ran to the swing at the back of the garden.

Tabitha grabbed the clue first and read it.

'If going places is your goal, use me, for I am ready to roll!'

'It's the car,' Art shouted.

Art and some of my other friends headed for the driveway. But Heidi and Gail ran towards a little red wagon.

'That's it!' I shouted.

'BOING-BOING!' Og agreed.

Heidi reached into the wagon and pulled out the next clue.

'A-tisket, a-tasket. The last clue's in a basket.'

I must not have been paying attention when Garth and his dad hid that clue. I looked out at the garden.

I was confused. So were my friends.

A.J. and Richie ran towards a large plant in a basket. But when they reached in, there was no clue.

Miranda hurried to Garth's bicycle, which had a wire basket on the front. But when she reached in, there was no clue.

Seth and Tabitha ran to a basket of fruit on the food table. They searched and searched but there was no clue.

My friends all stopped and looked around the garden again.

Then Art spotted a tiny basket

hanging from a low tree branch. He reached inside and found the clue, which he read.

'You'll find the treasure – do not worry. Look for something cute and furry.'

My heart went THUMP-THUMP-THUMP. This time *I* was the clue.

At first, my friends just stood there. I could tell they were thinking hard.

A.J. picked up Andy's teddy bear from a chair. He looked and looked but there was no treasure.

'Cute and furry,' I heard Miranda whisper to Sayeh.

Suddenly, Sayeh's face lit up. I call her Speak-Up-Sayeh because she's so quiet in class. But this time her voice was loud and clear as she said, 'Humphrey!'

Sayeh and Miranda raced to my cage. While Miranda looked on the outside of the cage, Sayeh opened the door and reached inside.

'Humphrey, do you mind if I look

in your cage?' she asked.

'Help yourself,' I said.

She gently poked around in the
bedding.

'I found the treasure!' she said as
she held up the chocolate coin.

Garth rushed to her side. He
was looking VERY-VERY-VERY
confused.

'That's not the treasure!' he said.

Garth reached into my cage and poked around some more. Then he turned to face his friends.

'The real treasure is missing,' he said. 'This is fake treasure.'

Sayeh looked unsqueakably
confused.

Garth looked unsqueakably upset.

I was unsqueakably sorry that
everybody was so disappointed.

Mystery Solved

'What did you do with it, Humphrey?' Garth asked me. 'Where did you hide it?'

'I didn't!' I squeaked. 'The thief took it.'

'Humphrey's just a hamster,' Garth's dad said. 'What could he do?'

'You don't know Humphrey,' Garth said.

Some of my friends laughed. They knew I'd had a lot of amazing adventures.

'Humphrey wouldn't do anything bad,' Miranda said.

'BOING!' Og added.

My other friends all agreed.

Garth shook his head. 'But how could the real treasure disappear like that? And how did the chocolate coin get into Humphrey's cage?'

'I'm happy with the treasure I found,' Sayeh said. 'Don't worry, Garth.'

But Garth was still upset. 'I don't know how that coin got in there. It was on my desk.'

'Do you think a thief came in and stole your treasure?' Garth's mum smiled. 'And then replaced it? That's silly.'

'No, it's not!' I squeaked.

'Somebody could have taken it while we were searching,' Garth said. 'We weren't looking at Humphrey's cage the whole time.'

'True,' Garth's dad said.

'False!' I said. 'You're WRONG-WRONG-WRONG!'

Everybody laughed at my squeaking. I wish they'd at least try to understand me.

'Only Humphrey really knows what happened,' Miranda said.

She was almost right. Og and I were the only ones who knew that the thief had stolen the treasure the night before.

She didn't know that we had no idea who the thief was.

I thought about who it could have been.

The only humans who were in the house were Garth, his mum, his dad, Andy and A.J.

Garth wouldn't have taken his own treasure. If he had, wouldn't he have told me?

Garth's mum and dad were too nice to steal anything.

A.J. wasn't a thief. But had he been playing a joke on Garth?

And Andy had been asleep in bed

when the treasure was stolen.

I looked at Garth's little brother.
He didn't look like a thief.
But he did look funny with
chocolate smeared all over his face.

'Andy! I told you, no chocolate
cake until later!' Garth's mum said
when she saw him. 'You sneaked
some chocolate last night, too.'

'Yum, chocolate,' Andy said. 'YUM!'

Garth said, 'Sssh!'

Andy said, 'Sssh!' right back.

The thief had smelled like chocolate. Andy loved chocolate. And he'd been eating it last night.

The thief had said 'Sssh!' Garth and A.J. said 'Sssh!' But Andy liked to say 'Sssh!' a *lot*.

Andy had been in the house last night. But now I knew he hadn't been in bed.

I raced to the front of my cage.

'You did it, Andy! You're the thief,' I squeaked. 'Turn yourself in!'

All my friends giggled at my

SQUEAK-SQUEAK-SQUEAKs.

But I didn't giggle.

'Andy is the thief!' I said. 'He did it!'

'Humphrey seems mad at Andy,' Garth said.

'Yes, he does,' Garth's mum said.

She turned to Andy. 'Did you take the treasure out of Humphrey's cage?'

Andy looked down at the ground.

'Yes,' he said softly.

'Why?' Garth asked.

'I like treasure,' Andy said.

Garth had another question. 'And did you put the chocolate coin in the cage?'

'I like chocolate,' Andy said.

It wasn't a real answer, but Garth didn't notice.

'Go get the treasure,' Garth's dad said. '*Now!*'

Andy went into the house and soon came back carrying the little treasure chest.

'Give it to Sayeh,' Garth's mum told him. 'And tell her you're sorry.'

Andy handed Sayeh the chest.

'Sorry,' he said.

He looked REALLY-REALLY-REALLY sorry, too.

Everyone gathered round while Sayeh opened the tiny chest.

'Oh!' she said as she reached inside. 'It's a gift card for Tilly's Toy Store!'

All my friends said, 'Oooh.'

Sayeh handed Andy the chocolate

coin. 'This is for you, Andy. Because you told the truth.'

Andy smiled happily, until his mum took the coin to save for later.

'Thanks for solving the mystery for us, Humphrey,' Garth's dad said. 'You're quite a treasure yourself.'

'BOING-BOING!' Og agreed.

'Og, you're a treasure, too,' Garth's dad laughed.

Garth's mum announced it was time for cake and ice cream so my friends ran off to the food table.

But Garth came straight back.

'Humphrey, I'm sorry I blamed you,' he said. 'I should have known that you'd never steal anything.'

He opened the door of my cage and put a small piece of carrot inside.

'Here's a treat for you,' he said.

Yum! That lovely orange carrot looked like sparkly golden treasure to me.

I hid it under the bedding in my cage for later on, when I'd have a treasure hunt all by myself.

'Thanks for making it a great party,' Garth said.

'You're welcome,' I replied. 'It was a GREAT-GREAT-GREAT party.'

And I REALLY-REALLY-REALLY meant it.

My Playful Puppy
PROBLEM!

I'd like you to meet some of my friends

Og

a frog, is the other classroom pet in Room 26. He makes a funny sound: BOING!

Aldo Amato

is a grown-up who cleans Room 26 at night. He's a special friend who always brings me a treat and seems to understand my squeaks better than most humans.

Mrs Brisbane

is our teacher. She really understands her students – even me!

Repeat-It-Please-Richie

is Aldo's nephew and a classmate of mine.

Stop-Giggling-Gail
loves to giggle – and so do I!

Speak-Up-Sayeh
is unsqueakably smart, but she's shy and doesn't like to speak in class.

Raise-Your-Hand-Heidi
is always quick with an answer.

Pay-Attention-Art
is a FUN-FUN-FUN friend!

I think you'll like my other friends, too, such as *Wait-For-The-Bell-Garth, Lower-Your-Voice-A.J. Mrs Brisbane* and *Don't-Complain-Mandy*.

CONTENTS

Pet Project

It was Friday afternoon in Room 26 of Longfellow School, where I'm the classroom hamster.

I was nibbling on a yummy carrot stick when I heard Mrs Brisbane say, 'Class, don't forget to bring in your science projects on Monday.'

That was such exciting news, I almost dropped my carrot.

My classmates had been talking about their experiments all week and they sounded unsqueakably interesting!

I turned to Og, the other classroom pet.

'Did you hear that, Og?' I said. 'We're going to see everyone's science projects on Monday!'

'BOING!' Og replied. He makes a funny sound, but he can't help it. He's a frog.

'Who would like to give us a sneak peek of your project now?' Mrs Brisbane asked.

'I would!' Raise-Your-Hand-Heidi called out..

'Heidi, what did you forget to do?' Mrs Brisbane said.

Heidi raised her hand. 'Sorry,' she said. 'I'm testing different liquids to see how long it takes for them to freeze.'

'Interesting,' Mrs Brisbane said. 'What have you tried?'

'Plain water, sugar water and salt water,' Heidi said.

A.J.'s hand shot up. 'I don't get it,' he said in his loud voice. 'Won't they be melted by the time you get to school?'

'Lower-Your-Voice-A.J.,' Mrs Brisbane reminded him.

'All right,' he said in a softer voice. 'But won't they melt?'

'Yes,' Heidi said. 'So I'm taking pictures and keeping a chart. That's what I'll bring in.' Just thinking about things that are COLD-COLD-COLD made me shiver, even though I have a fur coat!

'How about you, Sayeh?' Mrs Brisbane asked next. Speak-Up-Sayeh didn't raise her hand because she doesn't like to talk in class.

Sayeh smiled shyly. 'I'm growing beans on my windowsill,' she said. 'Some will have full sun and some will be covered.'

Stop-
Giggling-Gail
was growing
mould in her
fridge. Mould
sounded yucky
but Gail said it
was fun.

Pay-
Attention-
Art talked
about magnets
and Golden-
Miranda said
something
about making a
rainbow.

Then I noticed Richie Rinaldi waving his hand.

Mrs Brisbane asked him to speak.

'Mrumsum,' Repeat-It-Please-Richie said. At least that's what *I* heard. And hamsters have very good hearing.

'Repeat-It-Please-Richie,' Mrs Brisbane said. 'And this time, say it so I can understand it.'

'May I take Humphrey home this weekend?' Richie asked. 'I need him for my experiment.'

I was happy to hear that. Classroom pets like me *love* to be needed.

'I thought your project was about

ants,' Mrs Brisbane said.

'It was,' Richie replied. 'But my mum didn't like having ants in the house. Now I have a better idea using a hamster.'

Mrs Brisbane checked her list. 'Yes, Richie,' she said. 'It's your turn to take Humphrey home. Do you want to tell us about your new experiment?'

'Yes, tell us!' I shouted.

Of course, all my friends heard was SQUEAK-SQUEAK-SQUEAK.

Richie thought for a moment. 'I think it should be a surprise.'

Kirk Chen raised his hand. 'I know what it is,' he said. 'Richie's going to turn Humphrey into a monster!'

Then he raised his arms straight
up in front of him and made a scary
face.

'And when he's a monster, he can have a *ghoul friend*!' Kirk added.

Everybody laughed.

It was funny, unless you were the hamster who was going to be turned into a monster!

And I really didn't want a ghoul friend!

'BOING-BOING-BOING-BOING!' Og sounded unsqueakably worried.

After all, his tank sits next to my cage on the table by the window.

He probably didn't want to have a monster for a neighbour.

But Richie had a big smile on his face.

I was happy for him.

I would have been even happier if I'd known what the experiment was going to be!

'I have a surprise for you at home,' Richie said on the school bus that afternoon.

I slid from one side of my cage to the other because the bus is bumpy and thumpy.

'Just you wait,' Richie said. 'It's a giant surprise.'

A giant is something like a monster. Did Richie already have a giant at home?

'Eeek!' I squeaked.

Richie just laughed. 'You'll find out soon enough,' he said.

The surprise had a name: Poppy.

Poppy was a puppy.

She was small, with curly fur, and she *loved* to bark.

All that barking made my ears twitch and my whiskers wiggle.

'Isn't she great, Humphrey?' Richie asked as he set my cage on the desk in his room. 'I've wanted a dog for years and finally my parents let me have one.'

I didn't really think Poppy was a great pet.

I didn't think *any* dog was great.

Dogs have large, pointed teeth and wet noses.

They have big tails and sharp claws.

And they aren't usually friendly to small creatures like me.

'Woof!' Poppy barked as she tried to jump up and see me.

Luckily, she was too short to get all the way up to my cage.

'She likes you, Humphrey,' Richie laughed. 'She wants to be your friend.'

'Woof!' Poppy barked.

She even wagged her tail.

But I still didn't think she wanted to be my friend.

'Wait until Uncle Aldo comes over tomorrow,' Richie said. 'He's going to help me with my experiment.'

Richie's Uncle Aldo is also our school's cleaner.

At night, when he comes into

Room 26 to clean, he talks to Og and me. Sometimes he balances a broom on one finger and gives us treats.

I was glad I'd be seeing Aldo the next day.

I wasn't
glad about the
experiment, though.

Especially after
we watched a
scary film on
television later
that night.

Richie put my
cage on a high
shelf so Poppy
couldn't get near
me, but that didn't
stop her
from trying.

She looked
up at me

and barked and barked and barked some more.

'WOOF-WOOF! WOOF-WOOF! WOOF-WOOF!'

Richie's mum finally put the puppy in the kitchen so we could watch the film.

It was about a mad scientist called Frankenstein who created a monster. He hooked him up to a scary machine.

There was lightning . . . and the monster came to life.

He had a flat head and bolts sticking out of his neck.

The sight of him made my fur stand up on end!

Richie came over to my cage.

He made weird faces at me and said

'Humphrey-stein' in a creepy voice.

Then he laughed. 'Mwa-ha-ha!'
He didn't sound like Richie at all.

By the time Richie
brought me into his
room and went to
bed, it was raining
outside.

Would there be
lightning?

Would I end up
with bolts in my neck,
like Frankenstein's
monster?

Would people call
me 'Humphrey-stein'?

I crawled into my little sleeping house but I didn't sleep a wink.

I LOVE-LOVE-LOVE being a hamster.

But I would *not* love to be a monster.

I Go for a Spin

During the week, I get to see Aldo every night, but I hardly ever get to see him outside of school.

So I was HAPPY-HAPPY-HAPPY when he came into Richie's room on Saturday afternoon.

'Greetings, my fine furry friend,' Aldo said.

'Glad to see you, Aldo!' I squeaked.

'I think you're glad to see me, too,' Aldo laughed.

I love to make Aldo laugh because when he does,
his big, furry
moustache
shakes so
hard, I
sometimes
think it's
going to fall off.

'I hear Richie has planned an experiment with you,' Aldo said.

I didn't mind if Richie did an experiment *with* me.

I just didn't want him to do an experiment *on* me.

'Thanks for helping me, Uncle Aldo,' Richie said.

Just then, Poppy came racing into Richie's room.

'Whoa, slow down, pup,' Aldo told her.

Poppy must not have heard him, because she ran in a circle around his feet.

'Poppy, no!' Aldo said in a firm voice. 'Sit.'

Poppy did not sit.

Instead, she jumped up and put her front paws on Aldo's legs.

'Down, Poppy. Sit down,' Aldo told the dog.

Poppy did not sit down.

She wagged her tail and barked.

'You're going to have to train your dog,' Aldo told Richie.

'I will,' Richie said. 'But she's just a puppy.'

Just then, Poppy noticed me. She raced up to the desk and looked straight at me.

'WOOF-WOOF!' she barked.

'Go away!' I squeaked.

My squeaking only made Poppy bark more.

'Look!' Richie said. 'Poppy wants to play with Humphrey.'

The thought of Poppy playing with me made me shiver and quiver.

Poppy kept on barking. 'WOOF-WOOF-WOOF!'

Her voice was so loud, it made my tiny hamster ears hurt!

Richie's ears must have hurt, too.

He covered them with his hands and shouted, 'Quiet!'

But Poppy was anything but quiet.

'Time for you to go,' Aldo said.

He picked up the little dog and carried her out of the room.

Then he came back in without Poppy and closed the door.

'Now we can get to work,' he said.

'THANKS-THANKS-THANKS, Aldo!' I squeaked.

Aldo said, 'I think Humphrey is glad that Poppy's outside.'

Aldo is a very smart human!

Richie and Aldo pulled chairs up to the desk and looked into my cage.

'HI-HI-HI!' I squeaked.

'So, tell me what you want to do,' Aldo told Richie.

I scrambled to the front of my cage so I could hear Richie's plan.

'I want to see how many times Humphrey can spin his wheel in a minute,' Richie said.

I love spinning on my wheel, so that sounded GREAT-GREAT-GREAT to me.

'That's a good idea,' Aldo said. 'How are you going to do that?'

Richie shrugged. 'I'm not sure. He spins pretty fast. Don't you, Humphrey?'

I scampered over to my wheel and began to spin.

'Hey! Humphrey must have understood you,' Aldo said.

'But that's impossible,' Richie replied. 'He's a hamster.'

Aldo laughed. 'You never know with Humphrey.'

They both leaned in closer as I

began to spin faster and faster.

'I see the problem,' Aldo said. 'He spins so fast, it's hard to count how many times the wheel goes around.'

'Yes,' Richie agreed. 'Should I tell him to slow down?'

Aldo shook his head. 'No. Then it wouldn't be a real experiment.'

I kept on spinning while Richie and Aldo thought about the problem.

Then I heard a distant 'WOOF-WOOF!'

I had almost forgotten about Poppy, but she hadn't forgotten about me.

I heard her scratching at the door and barking.

'Go away, Poppy!' Richie yelled.

I don't think Poppy could hear him over all that barking.

She made me so jumpy, I spun the wheel faster and faster.

'Look at Humphrey go,' Richie said.

'I wish Poppy would go,' I squeaked. 'I wish she'd go far, far away!'

Aldo and Richie watched me spin on the wheel.

'You need a way to mark each time the wheel goes around once,' Aldo said.

I kept spinning and they kept thinking. I was hoping they had an idea soon, because to squeak the truth, I was getting tired.

'I know,' Aldo said. 'We need something that makes a sound.'

Whew! I was GLAD–GLAD–GLAD that Aldo had come up with an idea.

I let my wheel slow down a bit while I tried to think of something that makes a sound.

Luckily, Poppy wasn't making any sounds outside the door.

I looked over at the side of the cage where my water bottle and food dish are.

Sometimes my water bottle makes a GLUG-GLUG-GLUG sound.

But it's not very loud.

I looked over at my poo corner —
no sound there!

I looked down at my soft bedding.
It was nice and quiet.

Then I
looked up and
saw a tiny
little bell.

Not long
ago, my friends gave it to me for a
surprise.

I stopped spinning and hopped off
my wheel.

Then I scampered up to the top of
my cage and rang the little bell with
my paw.

DING-
DING-DING!
Aldo and
Richie were so
busy thinking,
they didn't hear
it.

I tried again.
DING-DING-
DING-DING!
This time,
Aldo looked up.
'What's that
sound?' he
asked.

Richie looked
up, too.

'Oh, that's Humphrey's new bell,' he said.

Aldo leaned in close to my cage. 'A bell? That's just what we need! Thanks, Humphrey!'

'You're unsqueakably welcome,' I told him.

Aldo probably didn't understand my squeaks, but I was happy he liked my idea.

Then Richie and Aldo went to work.

First, Richie took my wheel out of the cage and put it on the desk.

'Don't worry, Humphrey,' he said. 'You'll get it back.'

Aldo made a stand out of a coat hanger.

He hung the bell on the coat hanger with a piece of string and set it near the wheel.

'We need something that will ring the bell each time the wheel spins,' Aldo said. 'It must be strong enough to ring the bell but small enough to fit under the wheel.'

This time, Richie came up with a good idea.

Soon, they had attached a bent paper clip to the side of my wheel.

'Humphrey, we need your help again,' Richie said.

That was GOOD-GOOD-GOOD news, because classroom hamsters like me love to help!

Richie reached into my cage and gently placed me on my wheel again.

'You know what to do, Humphrey,' he said.

Yes, I did!

I began to spin my wheel, faster and faster.

DING-DING-DING-DING-DING!

Just then, Richie put his hand on my wheel.

I stopped so suddenly, I tumbled over.

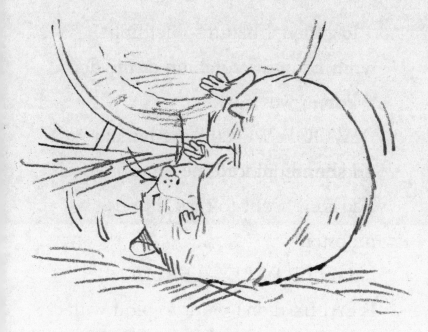

'Sorry, Humphrey,' he said.

As he gently placed me back in my cage, Richie told me, 'I need to finish the rest of the experiment.'

The *rest* of the experiment?

What was coming next?

Would I end up like the monster in the Frankenstein film?

Just then, I heard something
whining and scratching at the door.

Poppy was back!

'WOOF-WOOF!' she barked.

I shivered a little.

I didn't want to turn into a
monster.

And I REALLY-REALLY-
REALLY didn't want to play with
Poppy!

The Great Dog Disaster

'I know what puppies like,' Aldo said.
'I'll take Poppy out in the garden
and we'll play with her ball.'

Aldo is an unsqueakably nice man!

Things were quiet while Aldo and
Poppy were gone.

Richie quietly drew a chart
and began decorating a big board
describing his experiment.

'Poppy loves fetching that ball,'
Aldo said when he came back. 'I left
her in the garden for a while.'

That was GOOD-GOOD-GOOD
news!

Aldo gave Richie a stopwatch, so
he could time my spinning.

'Are you ready,
Humphrey?'
Richie asked.

He gently took
me out of my
cage and set me
on the wheel.

I started spinning, slowly at first.

Then I picked up speed.

'Ready, set, go!' Richie said as he
started the stopwatch.

I spun faster and faster.

DING-DING!

Each time the bell rang, Richie
made a mark on his chart.

DING-DING-DING!

I picked up speed.

'Go, Humphrey!' Aldo said.

DING-DING-DING-DING!

I spun so fast, Richie had trouble keeping up.

'That's one minute,' Richie said. 'Keep going, Humphrey.'

I can spin on my wheel for a long time.

And I liked the sound of the bell ringing.

Aldo took pictures of me.

'Smile, Humphrey!' he said as a bright light flashed.

'Two minutes,' Richie announced.

I kept on spinning and spinning.

After all, I wanted Richie to get good marks for his experiment.

I lost track of how many minutes I spun.

'That's it,' Richie said after a while. 'You can rest now, Humphrey.'

He slowed the wheel with his hand and then moved me back to my cage.

'I think Humphrey needs a nap,' Aldo said.

He was right about that!

'And I have to get home,' Aldo added. 'I don't think you need my help any more.'

As Richie said goodbye to Aldo, I burrowed under my soft bedding and fell asleep.

When I woke up, Richie was sitting at his desk, writing his report.

'How's it going?' I squeaked.

'Hi, Humphrey,' he said. 'You did a lot of spinning today.'

'I'm always happy to help,' I said. And I REALLY-REALLY-REALLY meant it.

Later, when Richie went to bed, his mum and dad came in to say goodnight.

'Will you be able to finish the project tomorrow?' his dad asked.

'Yes,' Richie said with a smile. 'I'm

almost finished now.'

When they left the room, his parents turned out the lights and shut the door.

But it wasn't long before I heard someone scratching and whining outside.

It was Poppy!

'Sometimes she sleeps in my room, Humphrey,' Richie said. 'But I think I should keep her away from you.'

'*Far* away!' I agreed.

Luckily, I heard Richie's mum say, 'No, Poppy. You'll sleep in our room tonight.'

And then, finally, it was quiet.

I slept well that night and so did Richie.

On Sunday, Richie did the last bits of his project.

By late afternoon, the report, the chart and the photos were up on the board.

Richie had used bright colours and it looked GREAT-GREAT-GREAT! My wheel with the bell and the clip sat in front of the big board.

'You did a hamster-iffic job!' I squeaked to Richie.

'It turned out pretty well,' Richie said. 'I just hope Mrs Brisbane likes it.'

'She will!' I told him and I meant it.

Once in a while, I'd hear Poppy scratching at the door.

Sometimes, she even barked.

'WOOF-WOOF!'

But Richie kept the door tightly closed, which made me unsqueakably happy!

When he was finished, Richie's whole family came in to see the project.

Richie put me on the wheel and I start spinning as fast as I could while he explained how it worked.

His two sisters and his brother were so excited to see me spin, I went even faster.

'Go, Humphrey, go!' they shouted.

When Richie made me stop spinning, his mum said, 'I'm proud of you, Richie.'

'I'm proud of you *and* Humphrey,' his dad said. 'Let's celebrate and go out for supper.'

'Sounds like fun!' I squeaked.

But it turns out that hamsters aren't allowed in restaurants.

Not even neat and polite hamsters like me.

Soon, I was alone in Richie's room. The house was quiet and I dozed off.

I'm not sure how long I was asleep before I heard a whining sound.

Poppy was outside Richie's bedroom door!

Luckily the door was closed.

I closed my eyes and tried to get back to sleep.

Then I heard a scratching sound.

'WOOF-WOOF!' Poppy barked.

The noise got louder and louder and the door began to shake.

I'm not sure what Poppy did, but suddenly, the door burst open and there she was!

She didn't waste any time.

She ran straight towards the desk,
jumped up on Richie's chair and
looked at me.

I had never been so happy to live in a cage!

But if Poppy could open the door to the room, could she also open the door to my cage?

She might figure out that my cage has a lock-that-doesn't-lock.

My heart was pounding.

'Stay away!' I squeaked. 'I don't want to play.'

'WOOF-WOOF!' she answered, wagging her tail.

Poppy put her front legs up on the top of the desk to try to get closer.

Suddenly there was a loud crash as her big puppy paws sent the wheel sliding across the desk.

The big board collapsed.

The bell went DING-DING-DING.

Luckily, the noise scared Poppy.

She jumped off the chair and ran out of the room.

I was HAPPY-HAPPY-HAPPY that she was gone.

But I was SORRY-SORRY-SORRY when I looked at the desk.

The pieces of Richie's project were scattered everywhere.

It was completely ruined!

And all because of that playful puppy.

'Oh, no!' Richie shouted when he returned.

His mum and dad ran into the room.

'What could have happened?' Mrs Rinaldi said.

Mr Rinaldi looked around the room.

'Richie, was the door open when

you got back?' he asked. 'Because I remember closing it before we left so Poppy couldn't get in.'

'Yes, it was,' Richie said. 'So I guess she must have done it.'

'YES-YES-YES!' I squeaked. 'Poppy came in and wrecked the project!'

Just then, the puppy raced into the room.

'Bad dog!' Richie said.

Poppy just wagged her tail.

'She's just a puppy,' Richie's mum reminded him. 'She didn't know what she was doing.'

I wasn't so sure.

Mrs Rinaldi took Poppy out of the

room and closed the door.

Richie and Mr Rinaldi sat down
and tried to put the project back
together.

The board was torn, so Richie
taped it back together.

He smoothed out his wrinkled
report.

'What happened to the bell?' Richie asked.

His dad began to search for it.

'And where's the clip?' Richie wondered.

He began to search for it.

They spent a LONG-LONG-LONG time looking for the missing pieces.

Richie looked on the floor.

Mr Rinaldi looked on the desk.

'The clip slid under the lamp!' I shouted. 'And the bell is under the desk.'

'It's getting late,' Mrs Rinaldi said when she came back into the room.

Luckily, Poppy wasn't with her.

'I've got to fix my project tonight,'
Richie said. 'It's due tomorrow!'

Mrs Rinaldi joined the search.

Finally, Richie crawled under the
desk. 'Here's the bell!'

'And here's the clip,' his mum said
as she lifted up the lamp.

I felt a lot better and so did Richie.

But when he tried to put the project back together, it didn't work.

He placed me on the wheel and I began to spin.

When the bell hit the clip, the bell fell off.

Instead of going 'DING', it went 'CLUNK'.

He worked on it some more.

This time, when the bell hit the clip, the clip fell off.

'Oh, I can't do anything right,' Richie said.

Richie's dad tried to help.

When he finished, the bell didn't fall off, but it didn't ring at all.

'Richie needs to get to bed,' Mrs Rinaldi said. 'Now.'

'I'm sure you can fix it in the morning, son,' Mr Rinaldi said. 'We all need some sleep.'

I know Richie didn't want to go to bed, but soon he was fast asleep.

I, however, was wide awake.

The moon glowed brightly that night and I could see the wheel from my cage.

I stared and stared at it all night long.

It was almost morning when I saw the problem.

Mr Rinaldi had fastened the bell too tightly.

Someone needed to loosen the string that held it onto the hanger.

And I was the only someone who knew what to do.

The Playful Puppy Returns

There was no time to waste!

I jiggled the lock-that-doesn't-lock on my cage.

The door swung open.

I was about to scurry over to the wheel to repair the bell, when Richie's mum knocked on the door.

'Richie! Time to get up!' she called out.

I hurried back to my cage as fast as my small legs would carry me.

After all, if I ever get caught outside my cage, someone might fix my lock-that-doesn't-lock.

Then, I could never get out and help my friends again.

Just as I closed the door, Richie jumped out of bed.

He yawned and said, 'Hi, Humphrey.'

I squeaked back politely as he came over to look at the wheel.

'I wish I could get that bell to ring,' he said.

His mum called from the hall. 'Come and have your breakfast, Richie. You're going to be late!'

'But I want to fix my project,' he replied.

'You have to eat first,' she said.

Richie sighed and left his room.

I knew if he was eating breakfast, he'd be gone for a while, so I opened the door to my cage again and hurried over to the wheel.

It wouldn't take long for me to loosen the string so the bell would ring.

Suddenly, I heard the pitter-patter of paws on the floor.

I looked up and saw that Richie had left the door open.

Poppy was heading straight towards the desk!

She whined and wagged her tail as she looked up at me.

'Go away, Poppy!' I squeaked.

She hopped up on the chair and stared at me across the desk.

I could see her shiny teeth, and this time I didn't have my cosy cage to protect me.

I glanced around and saw a pile of paper clips on the desk.

I threw them at her nose, hoping to chase her away.

Poppy growled, but she didn't move.

Then I remembered that Aldo had said that she liked playing with a ball.

I'd seen a little bouncy ball on Richie's desk.

I scurried to it and rolled it towards the edge.

'Here, Poppy – catch!' I squeaked.

The ball rolled off the desk and across the floor.

While the pup chased after it, I worked on loosening the string.

To my surprise, Poppy came right back with the ball in her mouth.

She hopped up on the chair and set

the ball on the desk.

'WOOF-WOOF!' she barked.

Poppy still wanted to play.

I took a quick look around the desk and grabbed a small ruler.

Using the ruler like a bat, I swung it and hit the ball hard.

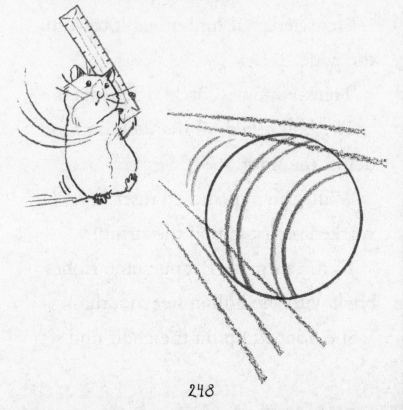

This time, the ball rolled much further away and Poppy chased after it.

I worked fast to loosen the string, but the pup came right back again and set the ball on the desk again.

'WOOF-WOOF!' she barked.

Her shiny white teeth looked SHARP-SHARP-SHARP.

I picked up the ruler again and aimed it in a different direction.

I gave it good hard whack and the ball flew off the desk and rolled under Richie's bed!

I heard Poppy's paws racing across the floor, but I didn't stop to watch her.

Instead, I stood up on my back paws and gave the string a good tug with my front paws.

Then I gave the wheel a spin and when the bell hit the clip, it rang.

DING-DING-DING!

It worked!

I raced back to my cage and closed the door behind me, just as Poppy returned with the ball.

'Sorry, Poppy. I don't want to play catch any more,' I squeaked.

It wasn't long before Richie came back to his room and got dressed.

'Richie! We're about to leave for school!' Richie's dad called to him. 'Get your project together.'

'What's the point?' Richie said. 'It doesn't work. Mrs Brisbane will give me a bad mark.'

'Try it!' I squeaked.

Richie walked over to the desk and looked down at my wheel.

'I don't understand why it doesn't ring,' he said.

Then he gave the wheel a spin and the bell hit the clip.

DING!

'I don't believe it,' Richie said.

He spun the wheel again.

DING!

'It works!' Richie grinned, giving the wheel another spin.

DING!

'I don't know what happened,' he said. 'But I'm glad it's fixed now.'

Richie wasn't the only one who was GLAD-GLAD-GLAD!

Once we got to school, Richie and all the other students in Room 26 set up their projects.

'Og, you're not going to believe what happened,' I told my froggy friend.

'BOING-BOING!' he answered.

Og sounded concerned, so I said, 'Don't worry, Og. It turned out well in the end.'

Then Mrs Brisbane asked my friends to explain their science projects.

It was unsqueakably interesting to learn from Heidi that plain water froze faster than sugar water. And the salt water didn't freeze at all!

Sayeh showed us the beans she'd grown.

The beans that had received the most light grew the best.

And the colourful mould that
Gail had grown in her fridge was
amazing!

Finally, it was Richie's turn.

He explained his experiment to the
class.

Then, he took me out of my cage
and placed me on my wheel.

'Why don't we all get a little closer

so we can watch?' Mrs Brisbane said.

I was HAPPY-HAPPY-HAPPY to start spinning.

DING-DING-DING!

The bell rang every single time the wheel went around.

DING-DING-DING-DING!

'Look at him go!' Lower-Your-Voice-A.J. shouted.

Golden-Miranda cheered me on, too. 'Faster, Humphrey, faster!'

'I think Humphrey needs a rest,' Mrs Brisbane said. 'But you've done a wonderful job, Richie!'

As the wheel slowed down, I looked up at Richie.

He had a huge smile on his face.

I think I had a huge smile on my face, too.

(Some humans think that hamsters don't smile, but we do.)

'Good job,' Kirk told Richie. 'But I still think you should have turned Humphrey into a monster!'

I like Kirk a lot, but I didn't agree with him.

I just want to be a helpful classroom hamster who goes home with my classmates at the weekend.

I love going home with my friends. *Even* friends who have very playful puppies!

My Really Wheely RACING DAY!

I'd like you to meet some of my friends

Og

a frog, is the other classroom pet in Room 26. He makes a funny sound: BOING!

Aldo Amato

is a grownup who cleans Room 26 at night. He's a special friend who always brings me a treat and seems to understand my squeaks better than most humans.

Mrs Brisbane

is our teacher. She really understands her students – even me!

Mr Morales

is the head and the Most Important Person at Longfellow School.

Lower-Your-Voice-A.J.

has a loud voice and calls me
Humphrey-Dumpty.

Golden-Miranda

has golden hair, like I do. She also
has a dog named Clem. Eeek!

Don't-Complain-Mandy

has a hamster named Winky!

Winky

is Mandy's pet hamster and one
of my favourite pals!

I think you'll like my other friends, too, such as
Wait-for-the-Bell-Garth, *Speak-Up-Sayeh*,
Stop-Giggling-Gail and *Pay-Attention-Art*.

CONTENTS

A Wheely Great Weekend

It was Friday afternoon in Room 26 of Longfellow School, and I was spinning on my hamster wheel, trying to stay calm.

Fridays are always exciting . . . especially for me.

Every Friday afternoon, I get to go home with a different classmate.

It's the BEST-BEST-BEST part of

265

my job as classroom pet.

Of course, Mrs Brisbane already knew whose turn it was, because she plans my visits with the parents.

But sometimes she forgets to tell *me*.

Who would it be this week?

Would it be Lower-Your-Voice-A.J., whose whole family likes to talk?

Or would I go to Speak-Up-Sayeh's house, where everyone speaks quietly?

'Mrs Brisbane, who is taking Humphrey home?' Heidi Hopper asked.

'Raise-Your-Hand-Heidi,' Mrs Brisbane told her.

Heidi forgets to raise her hand sometimes.

'I am!' Mandy Payne said. She forgot to raise her hand, too!

'That clock must be stuck. It's taking forever to get to the end of the day,' Mandy complained.

Don't-Complain-Mandy-Payne used to complain about a lot of things.

But since she got her own hamster, Winky, she doesn't complain as much.

'I can't wait!' I shouted.

My friends giggled, even though all they heard me say was 'SQUEAK-SQUEAK-SQUEAK!'

Just then, the clock hand moved and the bell rang.

The end of the day had finally come!

My friend Og splashed loudly in his tank.

He's a classroom pet, too, but he

doesn't go home with students at the weekend, because he doesn't have to be fed every day, like I do.

'I'll tell you all about my weekend at Mandy's when I get back,' I squeaked.

'BOING-BOING-BOING!' he replied, hopping up and down.

He makes a funny sound because he's a funny frog.

Soon Mandy's mum arrived to pick
us up.

'Humphwee!' a tiny voice shouted.

It was Mandy's little brother,

'Hi, Bwian,' I squeaked back.

His name is 'Brian', but he calls
himself 'Bwian'.

Mandy's younger sisters, Pammy
and Tammy, rushed up to my cage.

'*I'm* going to take care of you, Humphrey,' Pammy said.

'No, *I'm* going to take care of you, Humphrey,' Tammy said.

The girls are twins, but they don't look at all alike.

'*I'm* going to take care of Humphrey, because he's *my* classroom pet,' Mandy said.

It wasn't easy, but soon Mrs Payne had all four children, my cage, my food and me in the car.

It took *forever* to get to the Paynes' house.

Then, Mrs Payne had to get all four children, my cage, my food and me into the house.

That took even *longer*.

But at last, my cage was on a table in the living room, right next to Winky's cage!

'Hi, Humphrey!' Winky said.

When Winky was born, one of his eyes didn't open, so he always looks like he's winking.

'Hi, Winky!' I replied. 'How are things going?'

'Everything is hamster-iffic with me,' he squeaked.

'Same with me,' I said.

Winky is the only one I know who can understand my squeaks, because he's a hamster, too.

'Glad you could visit, Humph,' Winky said. 'Wait until you see my wheels.'

I looked closely at Winky.

He had four paws, just like me, but I didn't see any wheels.

'What wheels?' I asked.

'My car,' he said. 'The Paynes got me my very own car.'

I had a lovely, big cage, a wheel for spinning, a mirror, a little bell, and a hamster ball.

But I *didn't* have a car.

'Look at them. They're talking,' Mandy squealed.

Tammy, Pammy and Bwian – I mean Brian – all giggled.

'What are they talking about?' Mandy said. 'Oh, I know! Humphrey wants to see Winky's car!'

Before I knew what was happening, Mandy took Winky out of his cage and put him into a hamster-sized car.

It was bright blue and it had four wheels.

In the middle was a bigger wheel, like the wheel I spin on.

This was one really wheely car!

'It's unsqueakably wonderful!' I said.

'Watch this!' Mandy put Winky
in the big wheel and he started
spinning.

As the wheel spun, the car began
to roll.

Mandy took me out of my cage
and held me in her hand so I could
watch.

'Go, Winky!' I squeaked.

'Go, Winky, go!' Pammy, Tammy and Brian shouted.

Winky made the wheel go faster and faster.

Zoom! The car glided across the room.

Mandy picked the car up and turned it around.

Zoom! The car glided across the room in the other direction.

'Go, Winky, go!' Mandy shouted.

I think I have a wonderful life as the classroom pet in Room 26.

I think it's the best life a hamster ever had.

But I have to admit, I was a TINY-TINY-TINY bit jealous of Winky.

I wanted a really wheely car, too!

After a while, Mandy stopped the car and took Winky out.

'I don't want you to get tired,' she said as she put him back in the cage.

'Thanks, Mandy!' he squeaked.

Of course, I was the only one who could understand him.

'Do you mind sharing?' she asked Winky.

Winky squeaked. 'Not at all.'

Before I knew what was happening, Mandy put *me* in the car.

The car felt a lot like my nice yellow hamster ball.

But this was no everyday hamster ball. This was a really wheely car!

I started spinning on the wheel. Zoom! The car lurched forward.

Zoom! I spun faster and the car rolled across the room.

I spun faster and faster. Zoom! Zoom!

'Go, Humphrey, go!' Mandy shouted.

'Go, go, go,' Pammy, Tammy and Brian shouted.

I was going a little too fast, and the car slammed into the wall.

Zoom! The car spun around and rolled in the other direction.

'Isn't it fun?' Winky squeaked.

'It's the most fun I've ever had,' I shouted.

ZOOM-ZOOM-ZOOM!

I could have spun that wheel forever.

For the rest of the weekend, Winky and I took turns racing the bright blue car.

Sometimes Mandy put me in my hamster ball, so Winky and I could roll along next to each other.

It was fun, but my hamster ball doesn't have wheels.

'If you had a car, we could have a *real* race,' Winky said.

'I hope I'll have a really wheely car of my own some day,' I told Winky on Sunday night.

'I hope so, too, Humphrey,' Winky said with a wink. 'I really do.'

ZOOM-ZOOM-ZOOM Around the Room

'Og, there was a car and it was blue and I went ZOOM-ZOOM-ZOOM . . .' I squeaked to my neighbour when I got back to Room 26 on Monday.

'BOING-BOING-BOING-BOING!' Og jumped up and down in his tank.

'I'll tell you the rest later,' I said.

The bell rang and class began. Before our maths lesson, Mrs Brisbane asked Mandy to tell the class about our weekend.

'It was great,' Mandy said. 'I think Humphrey and Winky were happy to see each other. At least they squeaked a lot.'

My friends giggled. Stop-Giggling-Gail laughed the loudest.

'And Humphrey really loved rolling around in Winky's hamster car,' Mandy explained.

'Car?' A.J. said in his loud voice. 'He has a *car*?'

Mandy nodded. 'Yes. It's like a hamster wheel, but it looks like a car. Humphrey loved it as much as Winky does.'

'I've never seen a hamster car,' Pay-Attention-Art said.

'Me neither,' Heidi added.

'Well . . . I brought it with me,' Mandy said. 'Is it all right to show them, Mrs Brisbane?'

Mrs Brisbane smiled. 'Of course, Mandy. I'd like to see it, too.'

Mandy reached in her rucksack
and there it was. The little blue car!

'Oooh,' my classmates
said.

'Ahhh,' Mrs Brisbane said. 'Why
don't you show us how it works?'

Mandy gently took me out of my
cage and put me in the racing car.

She set the car on the floor and I began to spin the wheel.

'Go, Humphrey, go!' Richie shouted as I rolled the car between the students' tables.

I spun the wheel a little faster.

'Faster, Humphrey, faster!' I heard A.J. shout.

'BOING-BOING-BOING!' Og yelled as he splashed in the water side of his tank.

My friends all stood up to watch me, so I spun even faster.

I had a difficult time rounding the corner near Wait-for-the-Bell-Garth's foot, but I managed to keep going.

'I hope he doesn't lose control,' Mrs Brisbane said.

It wasn't easy, but I kept the car going without rolling *into* something.

'Humphrey! Humphrey! Humphrey!' my classmates chanted.

All their cheering made me spin even faster.

I spun so hard, I felt DIZZY-DIZZY-DIZZY.

Before I knew it, my car rolled up against the leg of Mrs Brisbane's desk.

The car bounced off the leg and spun even faster until it suddenly stopped . . . like THAT!

Mrs Brisbane had stopped the car with her foot.

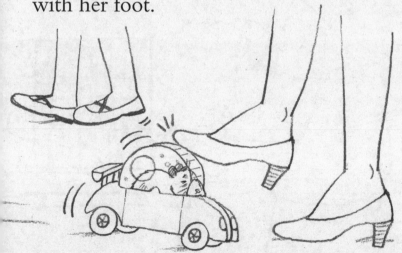

'Humphrey, I think you need a
rest,' she said.

I had to admit she was right.

'I can see that Humphrey had
a great time at your house,' Mrs
Brisbane told Mandy, as she put me
in my cage.

'Yes,' Mandy replied. 'I put Humphrey in his hamster ball and Winky in the car and they raced each other,' she said. 'But I think Humphrey would like his own car. Then they could have a *real* race.'

'A hamster race!' Garth said. 'I'd like to see that!'

'Humphrey should have his own car,' Golden-Miranda said.

'That's right!' A.J. said in his LOUD-LOUD-LOUD voice. 'They could race, and I know Humphrey-Dumpty would win!'

I like the funny nickname A.J. made up for me.

'Thanks!' I squeaked.

'BOING-BOING!' Og said.

When I looked around, all my classmates were smiling.

'Winky might win. He knows how to make his car go really fast,' Mandy said. 'But the car costs a lot of money. The only way I got Winky's car was by asking for it for my birthday.'

Money! Sometimes I forget about human things, like money.

My friends weren't smiling any more.

'We'll find a way. Let me think about it,' Mrs Brisbane said. 'Now, it's time to start our maths.'

It wasn't easy for me to think

about maths after all that excitement.

When Mrs Brisbane wrote an '8' on the board, it looked like a race track with fun twists and turns.

Later, while my friends studied science, Mrs Brisbane put me in the car and let me roll around Room 26.

It was fun, but not as much fun as being in my own car and racing Winky would be.

Even worse, at the end of the day, Mrs Brisbane gave the car back to Mandy.

'I'm sure Winky will want this,' she said.

'Yes,' Mandy said. 'But I hope Humphrey gets a car, too.'

'YES-YES-YES!' I squeaked.

'BOING-BOING-BOING!' Og took a big leap into the water side of his tank.

Mandy giggled. 'I forgot about Og. I wonder if they have frog cars.'

'Now that would be funny!' Mrs Brisbane said with a smile.

*

That evening, when Og and I were alone, I opened the lock-that-doesn't-lock on my cage and walked over to Og's tank.

'Do you want to be in a race?' I asked.

'BOING.' Og didn't sound very sure.

'Well, I do,' I said. 'And if there's a car for hamsters, there should be a car for frogs, too.'

'BOING–BOING!' Og seemed more interested.

I tried to picture Og driving a car.

With his big webbed feet, I didn't see how he could spin the wheel to make it go.

'Don't be upset,' I told him. 'I don't have a car, either.'

Og and I were quiet for the rest of the evening.

At least I could imagine having a really wheely car, even if it wasn't the same at all.

Really Wheely and Red

The next morning, Mrs Brisbane entered Room 26 with a big smile on her face and a large box in her hand. She said, 'Last night, I went to Pet-O-Rama.'

Pet-O-Rama? That's the pet shop where I used to live!

'I told the manager we want to have a hamster car race,' Mrs

Brisbane explained. 'And he wants to help us.'

The manager – my old friend Carl – wanted to help?

'YIPPEE-YIPPEE-YIPPEE!' I squeaked.

My friends looked as happy as I was.

The door opened and Mr Morales, the head of Longfellow School, walked in.

'Good morning, class,' he said.

He turned to Mrs Brisbane. 'What did you want to show me?'

'This,' our teacher said.

She picked up the box and opened the lid.

Then she reached in and took out a car.

It wasn't a real car.

It was a really wheely hamster car!

And it was bright red with flames painted on the side!

'Eeek!' I squeaked. 'It's just what I wanted.'

Mrs Brisbane told Mr Morales about Winky's car and the idea about a hamster race.

'Pet-O-Rama is giving this car to Humphrey,' she said.

I was so surprised, my whiskers wiggled and my tail twitched.

'It has the pet shop name on the back,' she said.

I scrambled to the tippy-top of my cage to get a better look.

It was true. 'Pet-O-Rama' was written on the back of the red racing car.

'Pet-O-Rama will also donate prizes for the winner,' she said.

I LIKED-LIKED-LIKED that idea!

'I'd like to see a hamster race myself,' Mr Morales said.

'BOING!' my neighbour agreed.

'Og!' Mr Morales said. 'What do you think of a hamster race?'

Og bounced up and down in his tank.

'BOING-BOING-BOING!' he said.

'We should have a frog race, too,'

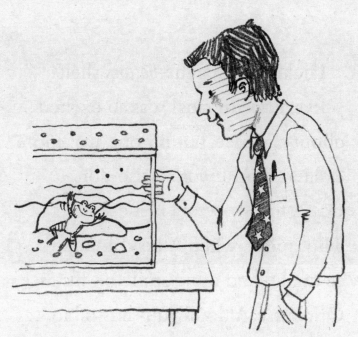

Mr Morales said. 'But I don't think they have cars for frogs.'

'Sorry, Og,' I squeaked to my friend.

'We'll make our plans tomorrow,' Mrs Brisbane said. 'Time to put this away.'

She took the red car and put it on a bookcase shelf.

Luckily, it was the *bottom* shelf!

Everyone in class was so excited about the race, but no one was more excited than I was!

★

That night, when Aldo came in to clean, he had a big smile on his face. Of course, Aldo always has a big smile each night he comes to Room 26.

'Humphrey! I heard the news,' he said as he pushed his cleaning trolley through the door.

'I hear there's going to be a racing day,' he said.

'BOING–BOING,' Og chimed in.

Aldo began to sweep the floor.

'That's one race I'm not going
to miss,' he said. 'After all, I have to
cheer for my buddy.'

'Thanks, Aldo!' I squeaked.

I LOVE-LOVE-LOVE it when
Aldo comes to clean.

But I have to admit, I was happy
when he left that night.

As soon as he was gone, I jiggled the lock-that-doesn't-lock on my cage.

The door opened wide and I scurried across the table.

'I'm going for a ride, Og,' I squeaked.

I slid down the leg of the table and ran across the floor to the bookcase.

There it was. The bright shiny red car!

I pulled myself up on to the bottom shelf of the bookcase.

I wanted to take it for a spin, so I gave it a little push.

The car rolled off the shelf and hit the floor with a BUMP.

It ROLLED-ROLLED-ROLLED across the floor.

'Wait for me!' I shouted.

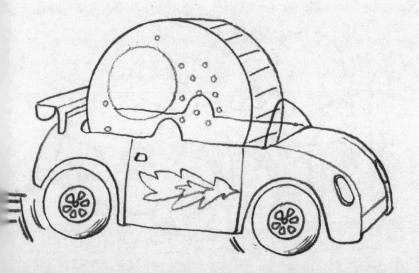

The car rolled between the tables in Room 26.

'Stop!' I squeaked.

'BOING-BOING!' Og sounded worried.

Just then, the car hit the leg of A.J.'s chair and it stopped.

'Thank you,' I said.

I stood up on my tippy-toes and popped the side door open.

Then I climbed inside.

'Here goes, Og!' I squeaked.

I began to spin the wheel.

The car started slowly.

Then I spun the wheel faster. And faster.

The car zoomed across the room.

'BOING-BOING-BOING!' Og cheered.

I thought about Winky racing next to me in his blue car, so I spun even faster.

I remembered that my car didn't have a steering wheel, so I couldn't turn it.

'Eeek!' I squeaked.

I stopped spinning, but the car kept on going until – BUMP! It hit the wall and stopped.

I climbed out of the top, which I hadn't been able to close with my paws.

'BOING-BOING-BOING!' Og leaped up really high!

'I'm fine, Og,' I told him. 'But I don't think I can drive the car out of the corner.'

'BOING!' Og dived into the water side of his tank and started splashing.

I have to admit, I was WORRIED-WORRIED-WORRIED.

Wouldn't Mrs Brisbane wonder how the car ended up in the corner?

Or what if she couldn't find it the next morning? Would she call off the race?

What if she found out that I had a lock-that-doesn't-lock . . . and then fixed it?

I could never get out and have an adventure again!

Then I had an unsqueakably good idea.

I squeezed into the corner and began to *push* the car towards the room.

UMPH! I'm a very strong hamster, but it was much harder to move the car that way.

I pushed for a while.

Then I rested for a while.

I pushed and rested for the rest of
the night.

There was sunlight peeking
through the window when I finally
got the car to the bookcase.

Of course, I couldn't push it up on
the shelf, but at least Mrs Brisbane
would see it there.

I scurried across the
floor and used the cord
from the blinds to swing
myself back on to the
table, as I've done so
many times before.

'I did it,' I squeaked as
I raced past Og's tank.
'BOING-BOING!'
Og said.

I pulled the cage
door behind me and
went into my sleeping
hut.

I was so tired, I
slept through maths,
reading *and* science.

314

After all, I'd had a LONG-LONG-LONG night.

I was unsqueakably surprised when I woke up and heard Mrs Brisbane say, 'Class, the great hamster race will be this Friday.'

'Eeek!' I squeaked.

'That's right, Humphrey,' Mrs Brisbane said. 'You'd better practise.'

She went over to the bookcase to get my really wheely car.

'What's it doing on the floor?' she asked. 'Maybe it rolled out when Aldo was cleaning last night.'

'Yes!' I squeaked.

It was a fib, but at least my lock-that-doesn't-lock was safe!

A Wheely Big Day

For the next few days, Mrs Brisbane
let me practise racing my car
around Room 26 while my friends
took spelling tests and solved maths
problems.

One afternoon, they made little
banners on sticks.

'We'll all be sure to wave our
banners to cheer Humphrey and

Winky on,' Mrs Brisbane explained.

'I let Winky ride his car every night,' Mandy said.

'Good,' I squeaked. 'May the best hamster win.'

As soon as I said it, I realised that in the end, Winky might end up winning.

But at least I'd give the race my *best*.

★

Friday was a very surprising day!

First, Mandy arrived at school with Winky.

She put his cage on the table by the window next to mine.

Winky had never been to school before.

After sitting through the morning lessons, Winky told Og and me that he thought being a classroom pet was unsqueakably wonderful.

'But I still love being Mandy's hamster,' he said.

Of course he did!

After lunch, Mrs Brisbane announced that the race was about to begin.

The whole class lined up and went out into the big hallway.

Mandy carried Winky's cage.

Miranda carried my cage.

'What about Og? He'll feel left out,' A.J. said.

'No, he won't,' Mrs Brisbane said. 'I have a surprise for Og.'

A surprise for Og? What could it be?

Some of the other classes from

Longfellow school were already lined up on both sides of the hallway.

Down the middle, there were racing lanes divided by rows of wooden blocks.

There were two lines taped to the floor.

One line was marked 'Start.'

The other line was marked 'Finish.'

Mr Morales stood by the line marked 'Start.'

He wore a tie
with little race cars
on it.

'Students, the
great hamster race
is about to begin,'
he said.

My classmates cheered and waved
their banners.

'Here you go, Humphrey,' Mrs
Brisbane said as she put me in my
really wheely car.

She closed the side and set the car
on the start line.

Mandy put Winky in his blue car
and set it next to mine.

'Good luck, pal!' I squeaked.

'Same to you, Humph!' Winky replied.

Mr Morales said, 'Ready, steady, go!'

Mrs Brisbane gave my car a gentle push.

I didn't waste any time in getting the wheel spinning.

I kept my eyes straight ahead as I spun faster and faster.

'Humphrey, you're ahead!' the students chanted.

'Faster, Winky! You can win!' they cheered.

I looked back.

Yes, I was ahead, but Winky was close behind me.

I spun my wheel even faster.

And then a terrible thing happened.

I was spinning as fast as I could, but my really wheely car wasn't moving!

It had rolled up against a wooden block.

I was stuck!

I heard people moaning. 'Oh, no, Humphrey!'

I heard the crowd shout, 'Go, Winky! There's the finish line!'

Winky was going to win.

I spun and spun but the car didn't budge, so I did the only thing I could.

I reached over and pushed the side door of the car as hard as I could.

Success! The door opened and I
crawled out of the car.

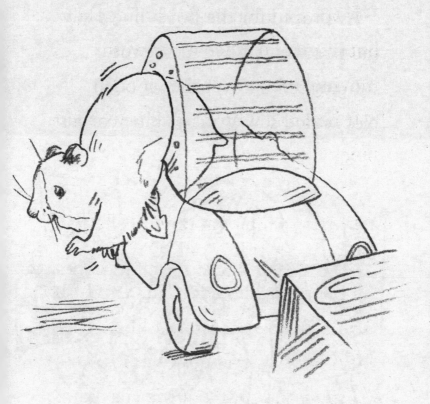

Maybe I couldn't win the race in
my car, but I could still cross the line
first!

The cheering got louder and louder.

As I raced for the finish line, I saw the banners waving above me.

I glanced up over the wooden blocks and saw Winky's blue car just

inches ahead of me.

I ran and ran as fast as my paws could carry me and I passed the blue car!

The finish line was right in front of me, so I sprinted across it.

Winky's blue car crossed the line a few seconds later.

I had won!

Or so I thought.

'Humphrey! Humphrey! Humphrey!' the crowd cheered.

Mrs Brisbane scooped me up and held me in her hand.

'Quiet, everyone!' Mr Morales said.

Since he is the Most Important Person at Longfellow School, the crowd quietened down.

'Humphrey crossed the finish line first,' he said. 'But he wasn't in his car. This was a hamster car race, so I think Winky is the winner.'

'No!' I heard some students say.

'Winky was the first hamster to cross the line in his car,' he said.

'But Humphrey was so smart,' Golden-Miranda said. 'He knew he was stuck and he still found a way to win.'

Mr Morales nodded. 'That's true,' he said. 'And I'm proud of Humphrey. But I still think that Winky won.'

'I have an idea,' another voice said.

I knew that voice.

Aldo stepped forward.

'What if we call it a tie?' he asked.

Mr Morales thought. 'We could do that,' he said.

Suddenly everyone began to cheer.

'Tie! Tie! Tie!'

Mr Morales raised both hands to quieten them down.

'All right,' he said. 'I think we can call this a tie. Is that all right with you, Mandy?'

'They both did a great job,' Mandy said. 'Winky is my pet and Humphrey is my classroom's pet. So I think . . . it's a tie!'

The cheering was so loud, it hurt my small hamster ears.

'Humphrey and Winky will each receive a First Place certificate *and* a box of Hamster Chew-Chews from Pet-O-Rama,' Mr Morales said.

I LOVE-LOVE-LOVE Hamster Chew-Chews.

The crowd got noisy again, but Mr Morales raised his hands.

'We have one more contest this afternoon,' he said. 'Longfellow School has two classroom frogs, so we're going to have a frog-jumping contest.

'BOING-BOING-BOING!' I heard Og say.

The crowd cheered.

'George is the classroom pet in Miss Loomis's class,' he said. 'Og is the pet in Mrs Brisbane's class. We're going to place them each at the starting line and see which one can jump the furthest.'

I remembered George! He was the reason that Og came to Room 26 in the first place.

Og was in Miss Loomis's class along with George, but George didn't like Og.

Since George was a huge bullfrog with a BIG-BIG-BIG voice, he made so much noise that Miss Loomis couldn't teach her class.

She gave Og to Room 26 and he's been here ever since.

'BOING-BOING-BOING!' Og shouted.

I could tell he was ready for the frog-jumping contest.

Miss Loomis set George down on the starting line.

Mrs Brisbane set Og down in his lane.

Og had a nice smile on his face.

George had a mean leer on his face.

And he was HUGE.

Could Og jump further than a great big bullfrog?

Mr Morales said, 'Ready, steady, jump!'

Miss Loomis let go of George and Mrs Brisbane let go of Og.

Nothing happened at first.

George sat on the starting line and so did Og.

Suddenly, George took a giant leap forward.

The crowd cheered, but Og didn't budge.

'Go on, Og! You can win,' I squeaked.

Og still didn't move.

'Go, Og, go!' the students chanted.

I was WORRIED-WORRIED-

WORRIED until suddenly, George
let out an unsqueakably loud noise.

'RUM-RUM-RUM!' he bellowed
in his deep, loud voice.

And then Og did it!

He took a huge leap forward.

He leaped past George.

Then he leaped again. And again!

'OG-OG-OG!' the crowd cheered

'Yay, Og!' I squeaked. 'I knew you
could do it.'

I wasn't sure he heard me until I heard him answer, 'BOING-BOING-BOING-BOING!'

'The winner is Og,' Mr Morales said. 'He will receive a jar of Froggy

Fish Sticks from Pet-O-Rama.'

Luckily, George didn't argue.

'BOING-BOING-BOING!' Og twanged.

'I want to thank you all for our very first Racing Day,' Mr Morales said. 'I think Longfellow School has the best classroom pets in the world.'

'Yes!' I squeaked.

Winky and Og were GREAT-GREAT-GREAT pets.

I tried hard to be a great pet, too.

I'm not so sure about George.

★

At the end of the day, Mrs Brisbane made an announcement.

'This week, I haven't assigned a student to take Humphrey home for the weekend,' she said.

'Eeek!' I squeaked.

After all, I love going home with students at the weekend.

'Instead, I'm taking Humphrey and Og home with *me*,' she said. 'They deserve a good rest.'

I love going home with Mrs Brisbane.

I love it when Og can come, too.

The day had been full of surprises, but this was the best one of all.

'Doesn't that sound like fun, Og?' I squeaked to my friend.

'BOING-BOING-BOING-BOING-BOING!' he replied.

I knew exactly what he meant.

Turn over for more
fun with Humphrey . . .

Want more Tiny Tales?
Try my first Bumper Book
– including:

My Mixed-Up Magic Trick!
My Pet Show Panic!
My Summer Fair Surprise!
My Creepy-Crawly Camping Adventure!

Bumper Book of

Humphrey's
Tiny Tales

Includes
a brand
new
story!

Humphrey's Tiny Tales

4 stories
in
1 book!

Betty G. Birney

Look out for my book of
unsqueakably funny jokes

Or why not try the
puzzles and games in my
fun-fun-fun activity
books?

There's one
for summer . . .

Puzzles
and
Games!

Humphrey's
Book of
Summer Fun

Betty G. Birney

ff

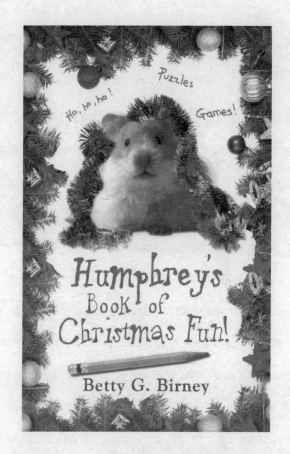

Puzzles

Ho, ho, ho!

Games!

Humphrey's Book of Christmas Fun!

Betty G. Birney

. . . and one for Christmas!

Dear friends,

Humans love their pets, and pets like me love their humans. I'm unsqueakably excited to share everything I've learned in Classroom 26 and beyond about the world of pets with you.

And hamsters aren't the only pets! Do you know how to look after a chinchilla? What is a puppy's favourite food? As well as learning top pet-care tips, you can tell me all about your pets in the special My Precious Pet section. I can't wait to meet them!

Your furry friend,

Humphrey

PET-tastic facts

WOOF!

LOTS of fun inside!

Humphrey's World of Pets

Betty G. Birney

Humphrey and his friends have been hard at work making a brand new FUN-FUN-FUN website just for you!

Play Humphrey's exciting new game, share your pet pictures, find fun crafts and activities, read Humphrey's very own diary and discover all the latest news from your favourite furry friend at:

www.funwithhumphrey.com